This translation has been published with the financial support of NORLA, Norwegian Literature Abroad.

First English-language edition, published in 2022 by Enchanted Lion Books
248 Creamer Street, Studio 4, Brooklyn, NY 11231
Originally published in Norway in 2016 as *Fuglefrakken*
Copyright © 2016 by Gyldendal Norsk Forlag AS – Gyldendal Barn & Ungdom
English-language translation copyright © 2022 by Kari Dickson
Design for the English-language edition by Emma Vitoria
All rights reserved under International and Pan-American Copyright Conventions
A CIP record is on file with the Library of Congress

ISBN: 978-1-59270-366-1

Printed in China by RR Donnelley Asia Printing Solutions Ltd.
First Printing

Inger Marie Kjølstadmyr & Øyvind Torseter
Translated from Norwegian by Kari Dickson

THE BIRD COAT

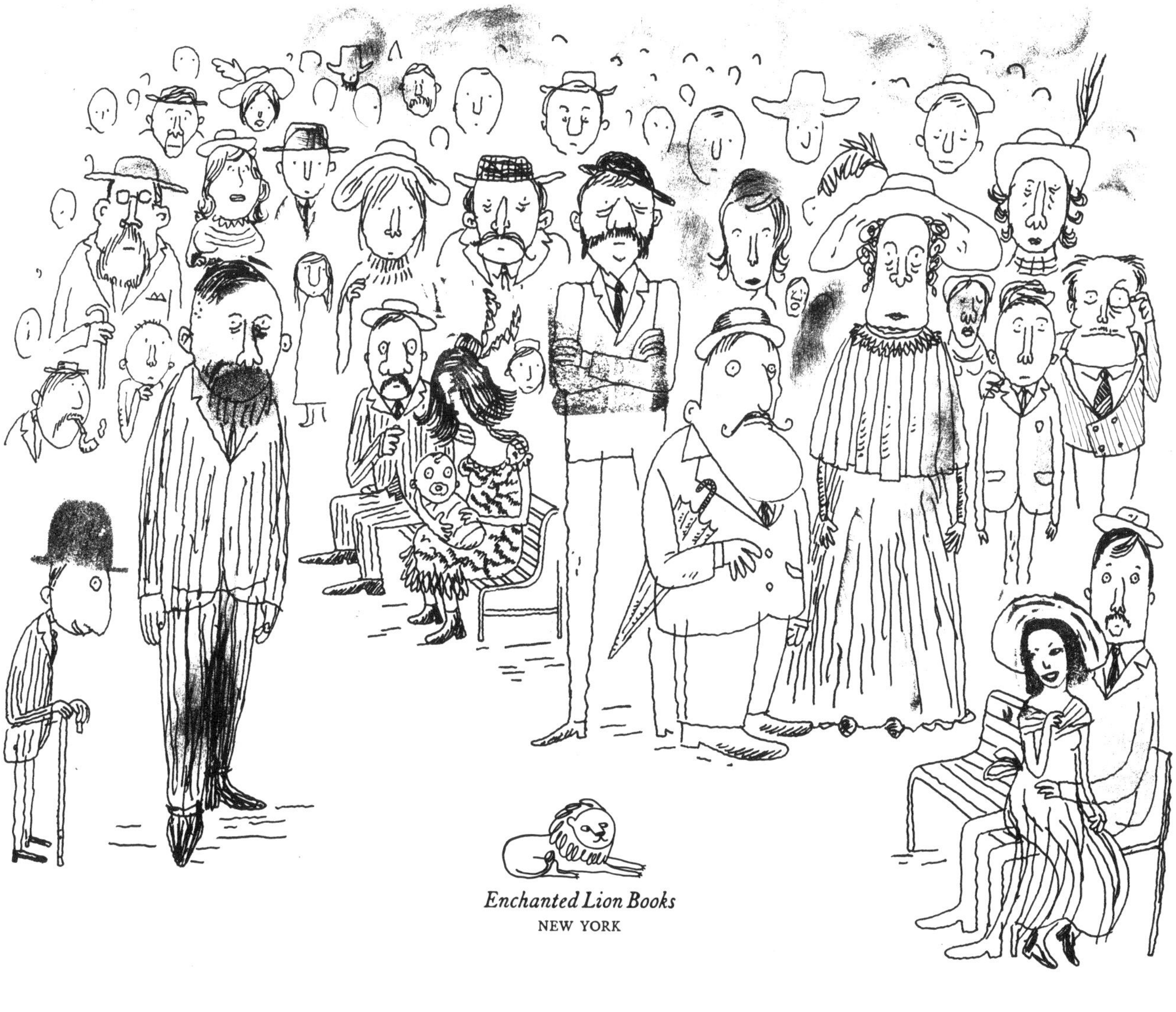

Enchanted Lion Books
NEW YORK

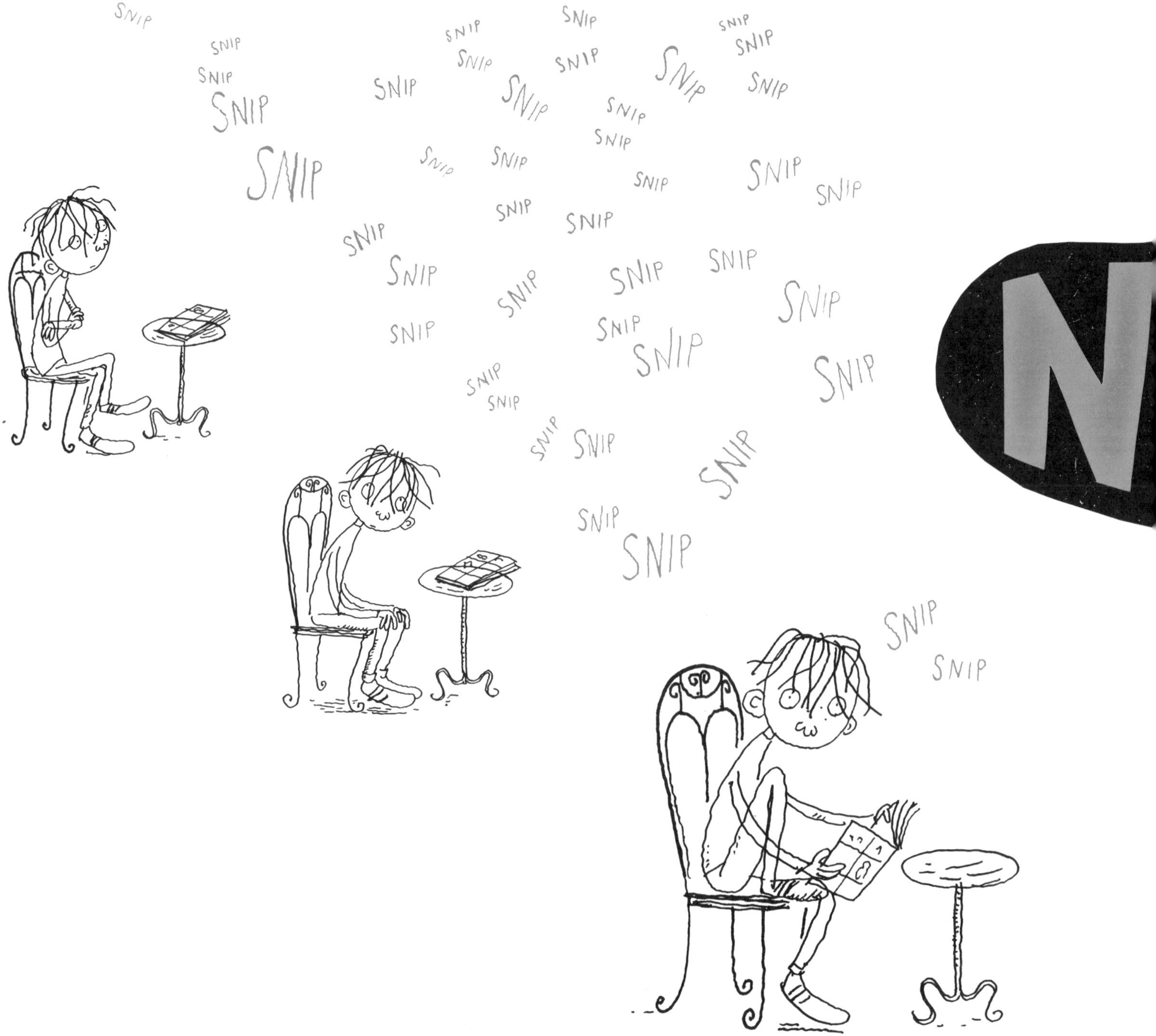
SNIP
SNIP
SNIP
SNIP
SNIP
SNIP
SNIP
SNIP
SNIP
SNIP
SNIP
SNIP
SNIP
SNIP
SNIP
SNIP
SNIP
SNIP
SNIP
SNIP
SNIP
SNIP
SNIP
SNIP
SNIP
SNIP
SNIP
SNIP
SNIP
SNIP
SNIP
SNIP
SNIP
SNIP
SNIP
SNIP
SNIP
SNIP
SNIP
SNIP
SNIP
SNIP
SNIP
N

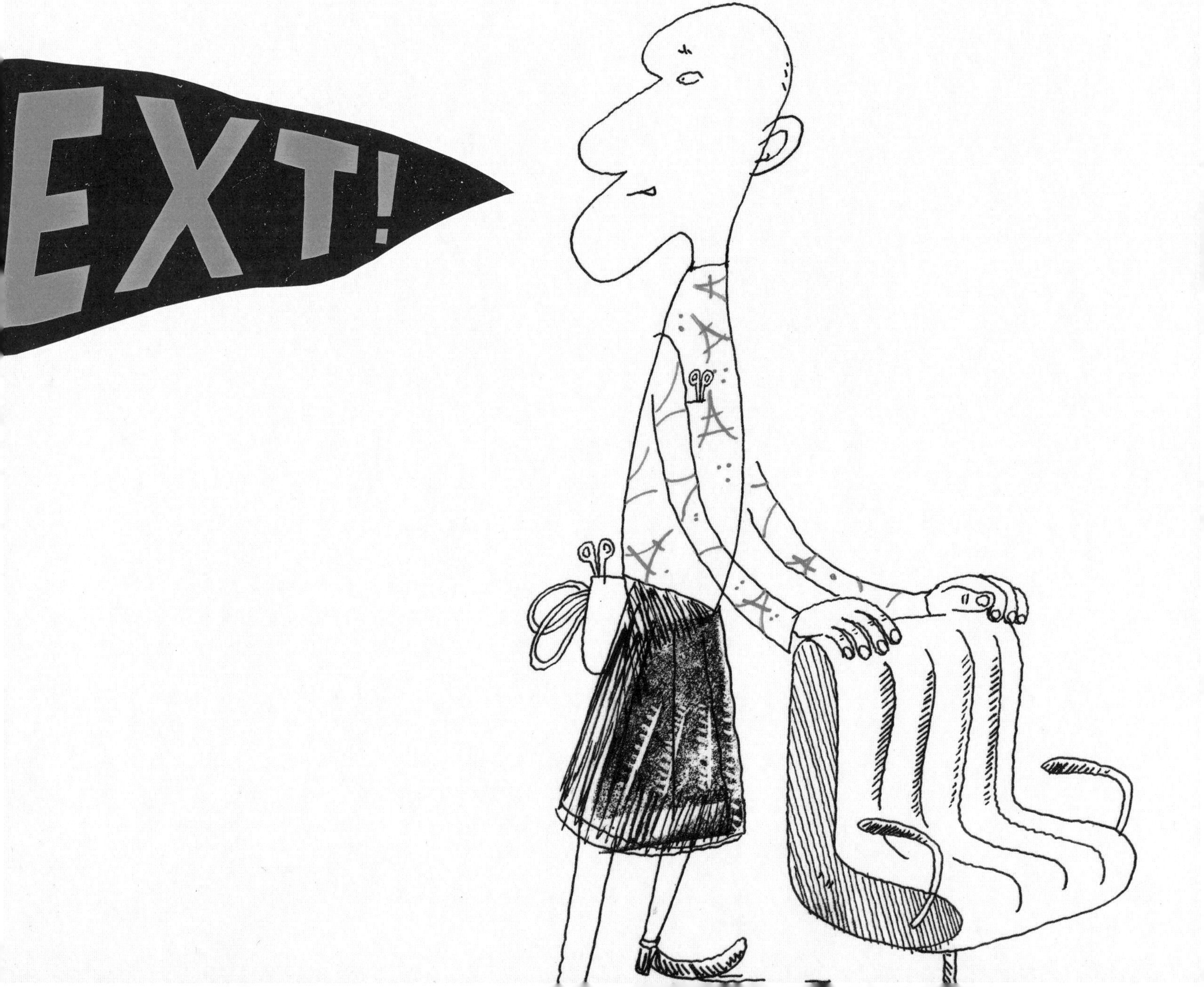
EXT!

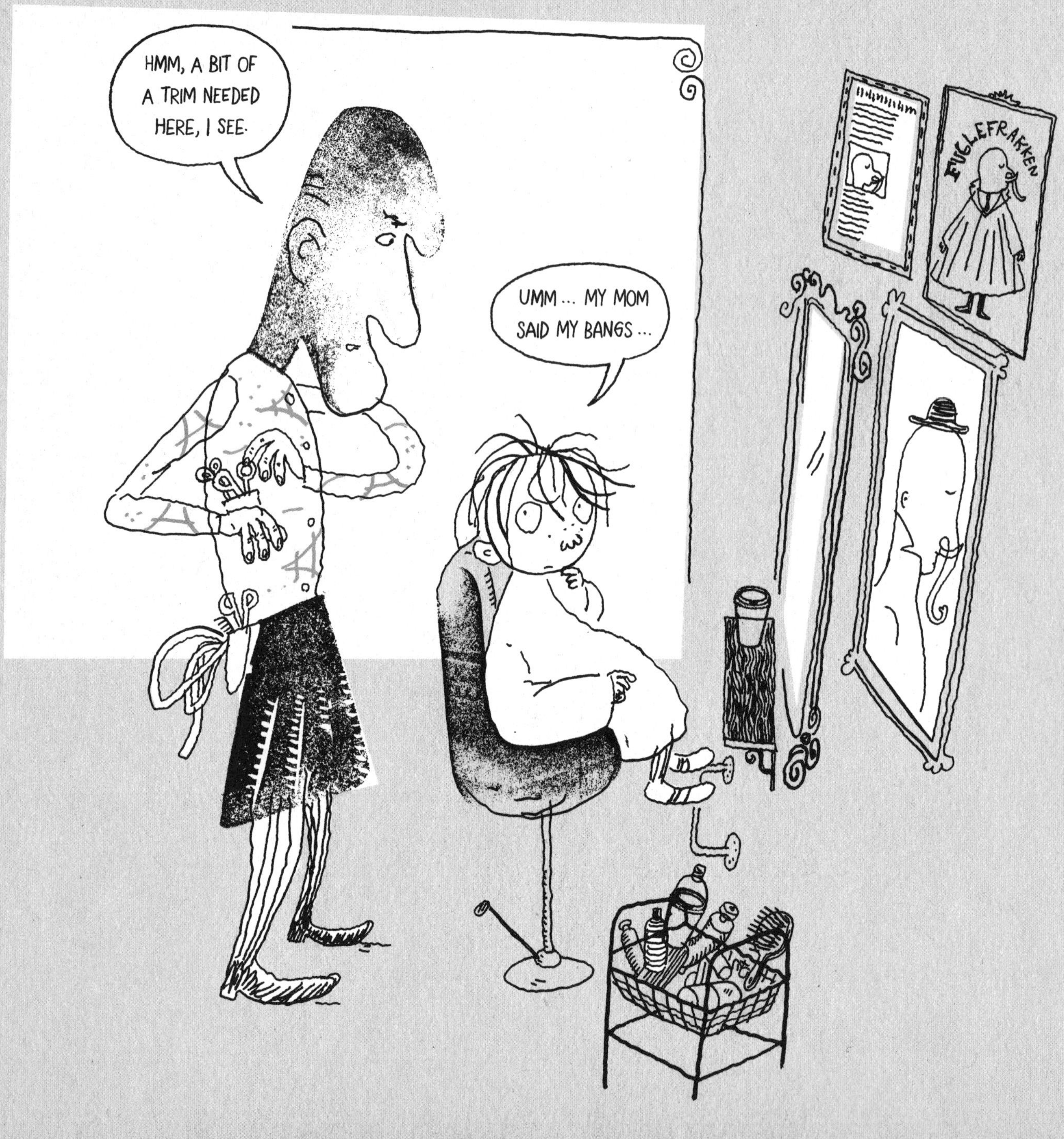
HMM, A BIT OF A TRIM NEEDED HERE, I SEE.
UMM ... MY MOM SAID MY BANGS ...
FUGLEFRAKKEN

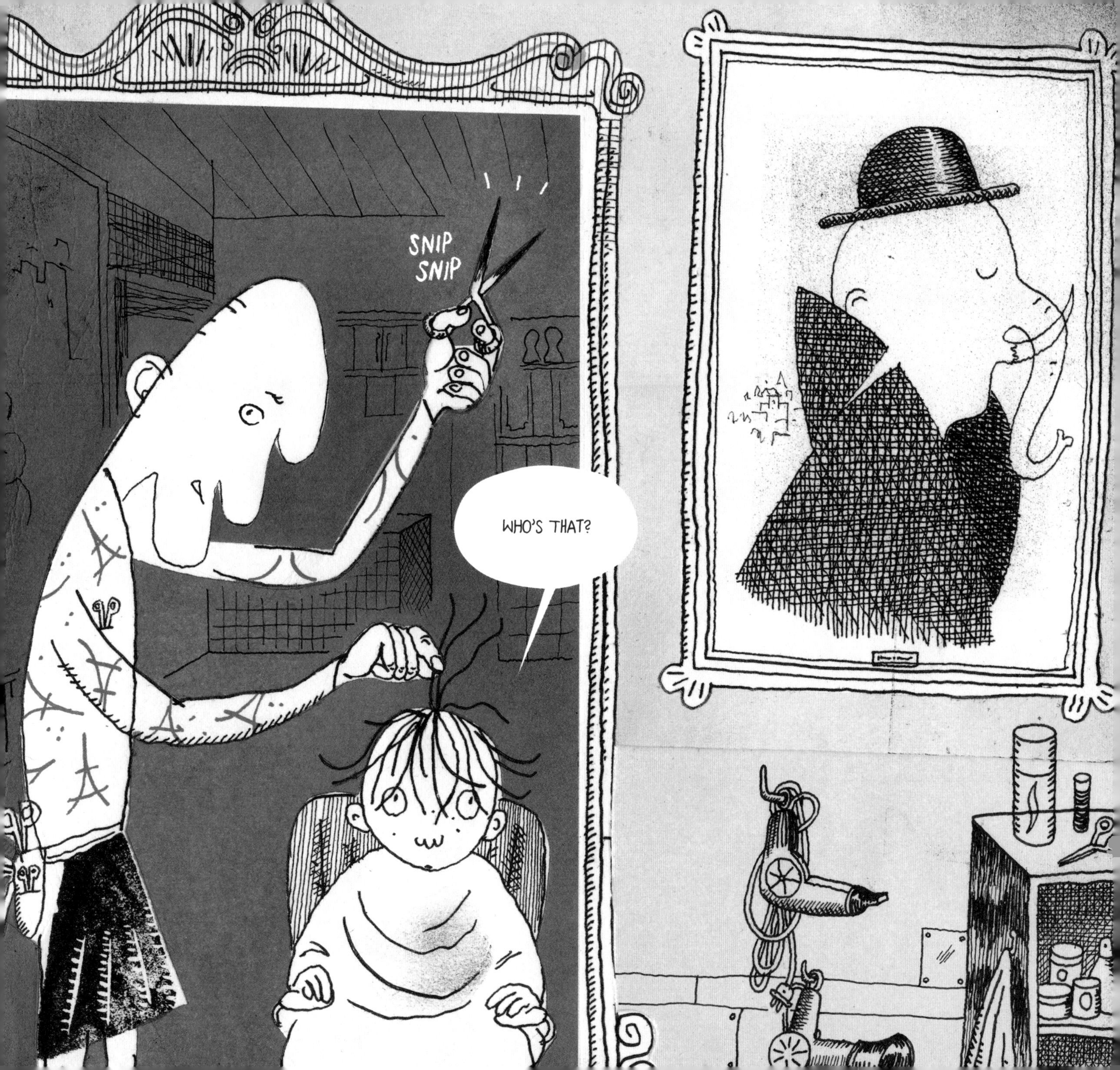
SNIP
SNIP
WHO'S THAT?

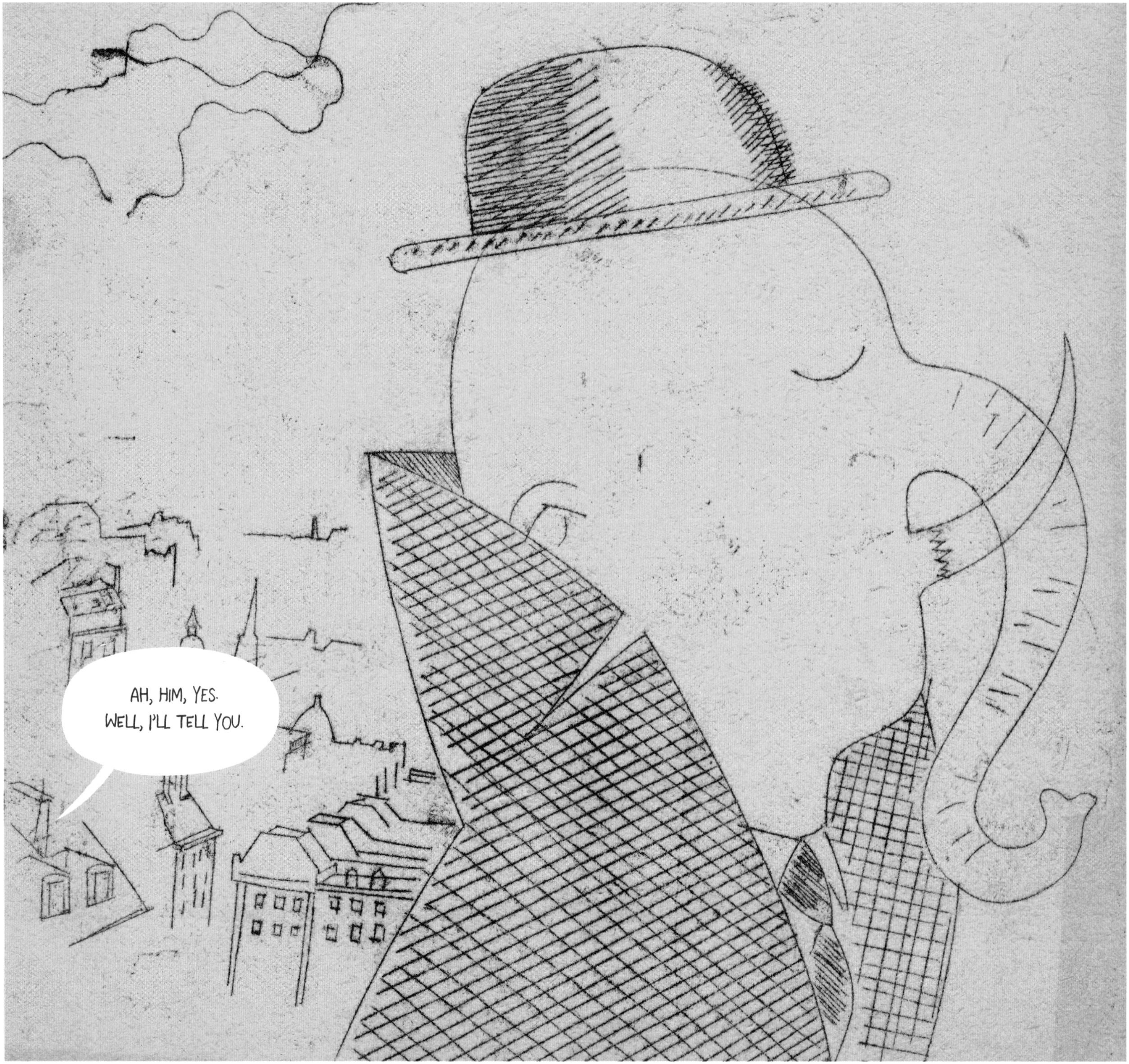
AH, HIM, YES.
WELL, I'LL TELL YOU.

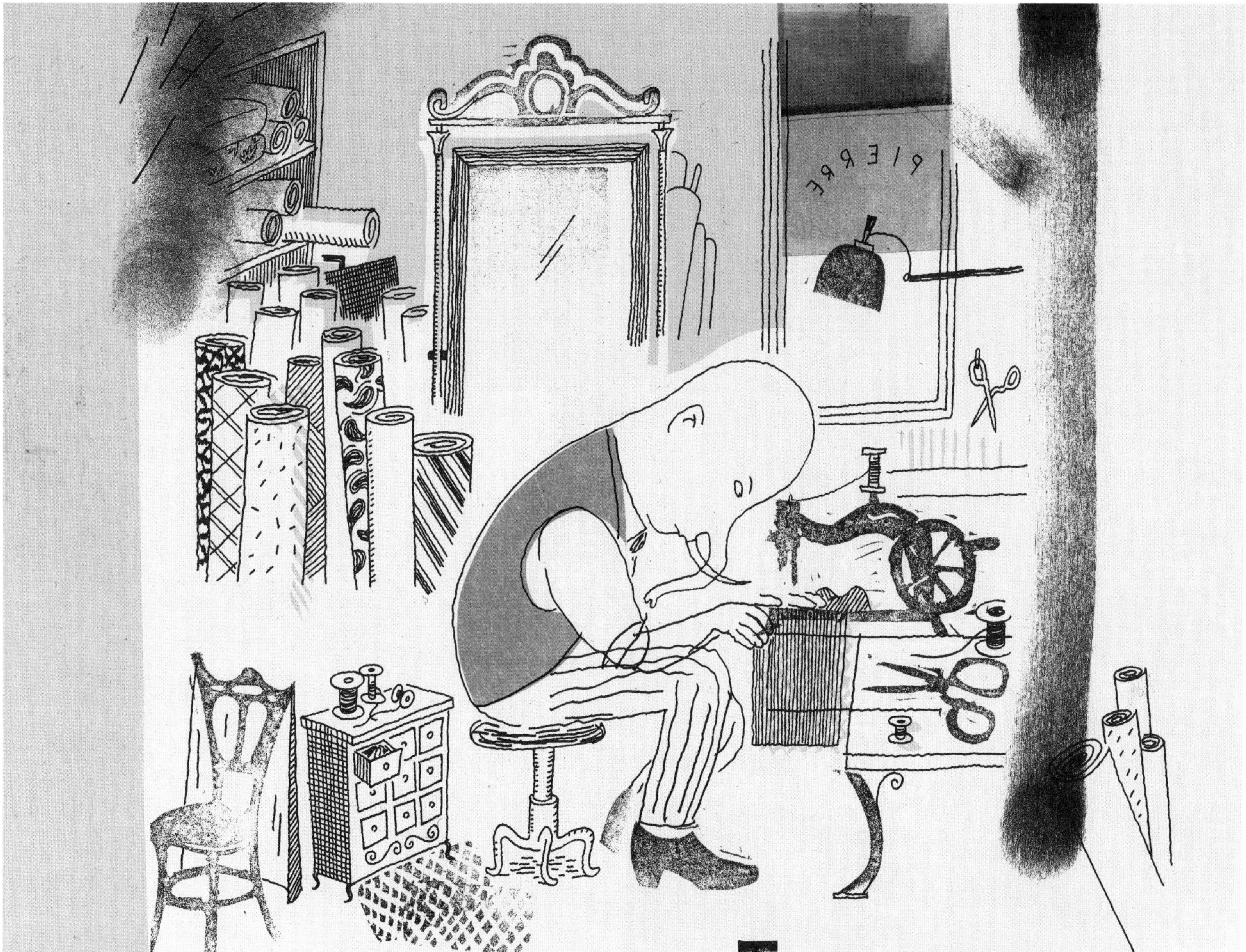
PIERRE

That is a tailor named Pierre. He lived in Paris, not far from here. His shop stood between a barber and a baker.

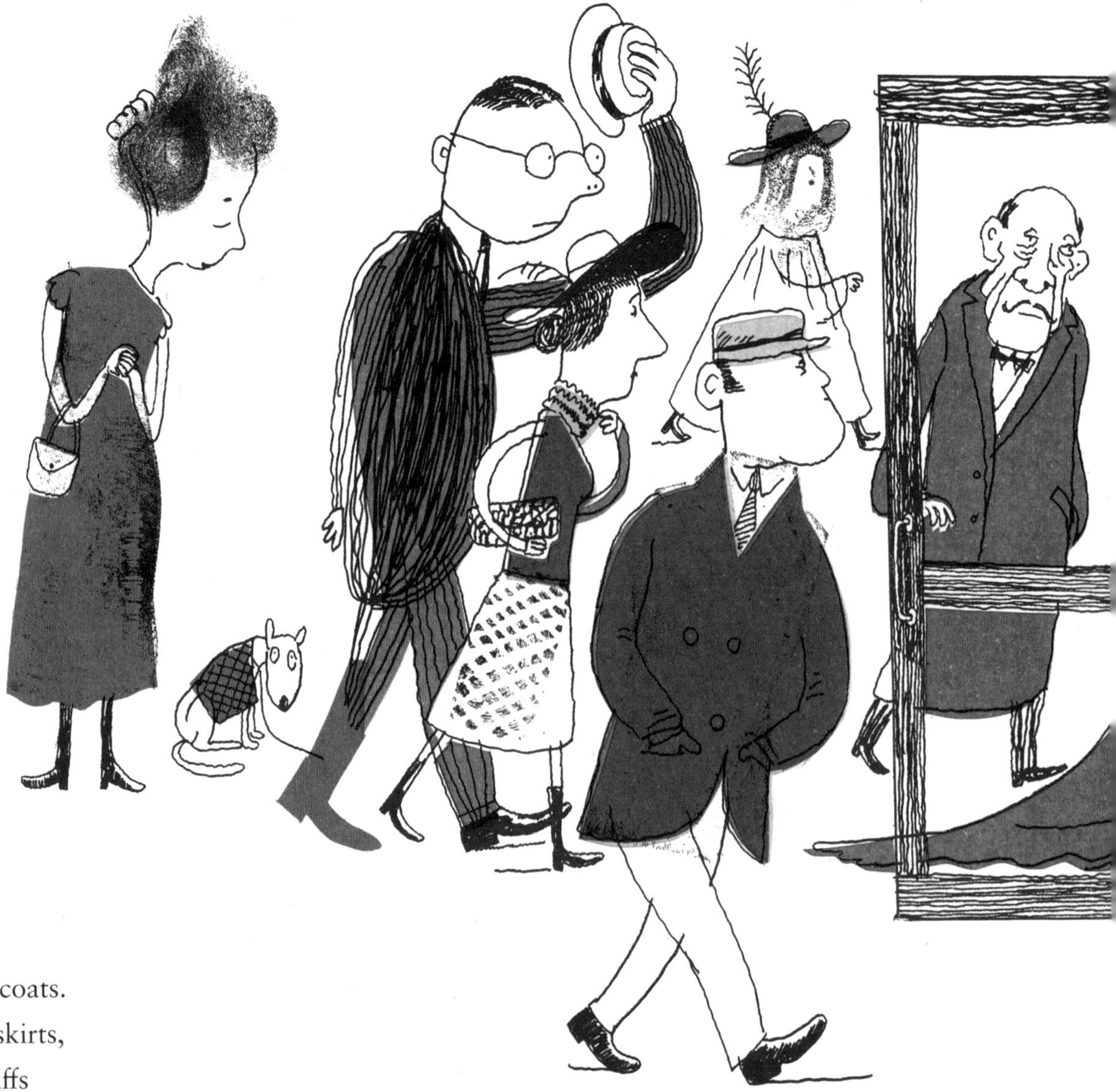

Pierre made winter coats.
He made dresses and skirts,
and he repaired the cuffs
of old shirts.

Pierre was a popular tailor.
So popular that sometimes
people had to line up all the
way around the block.

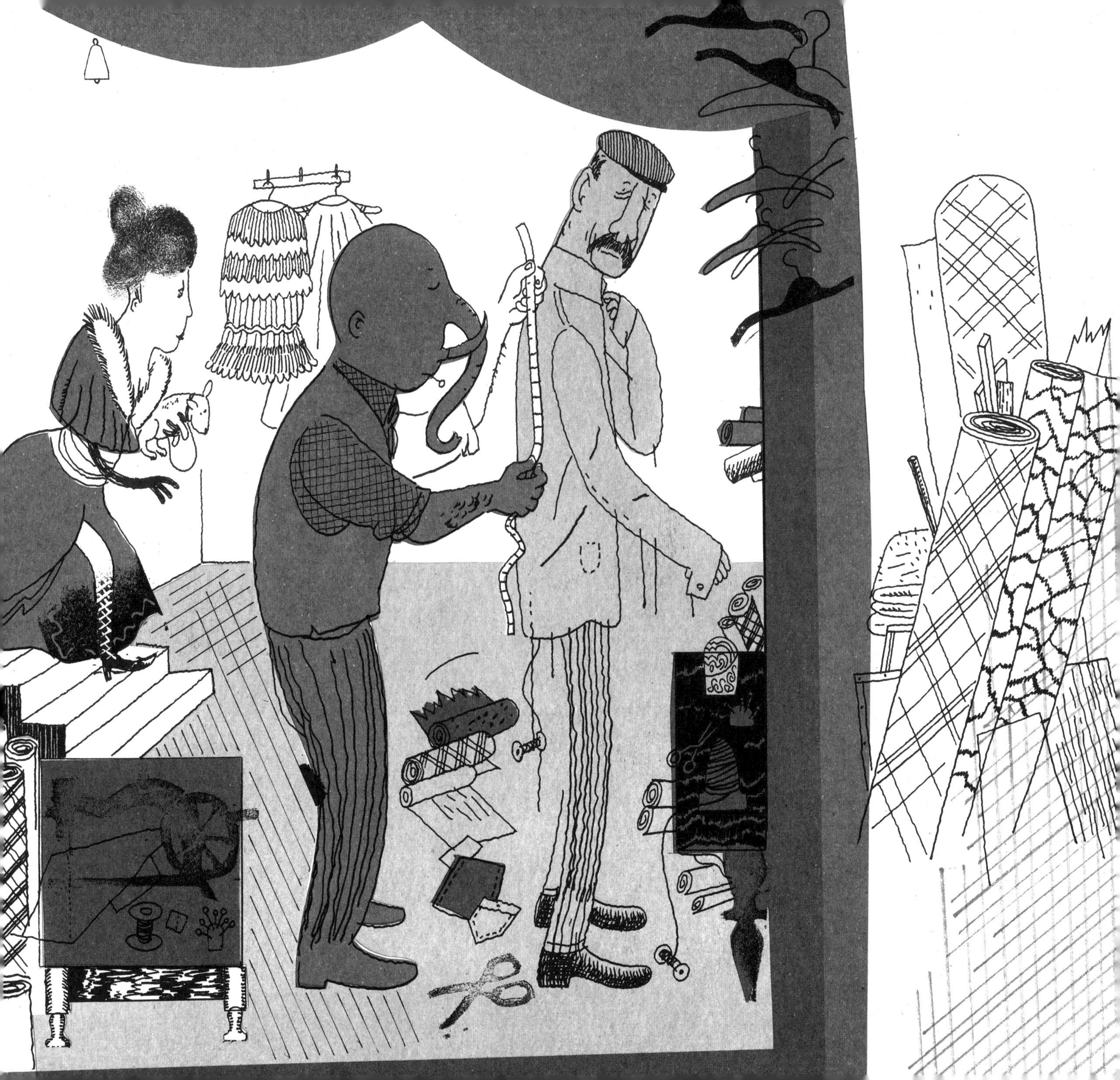

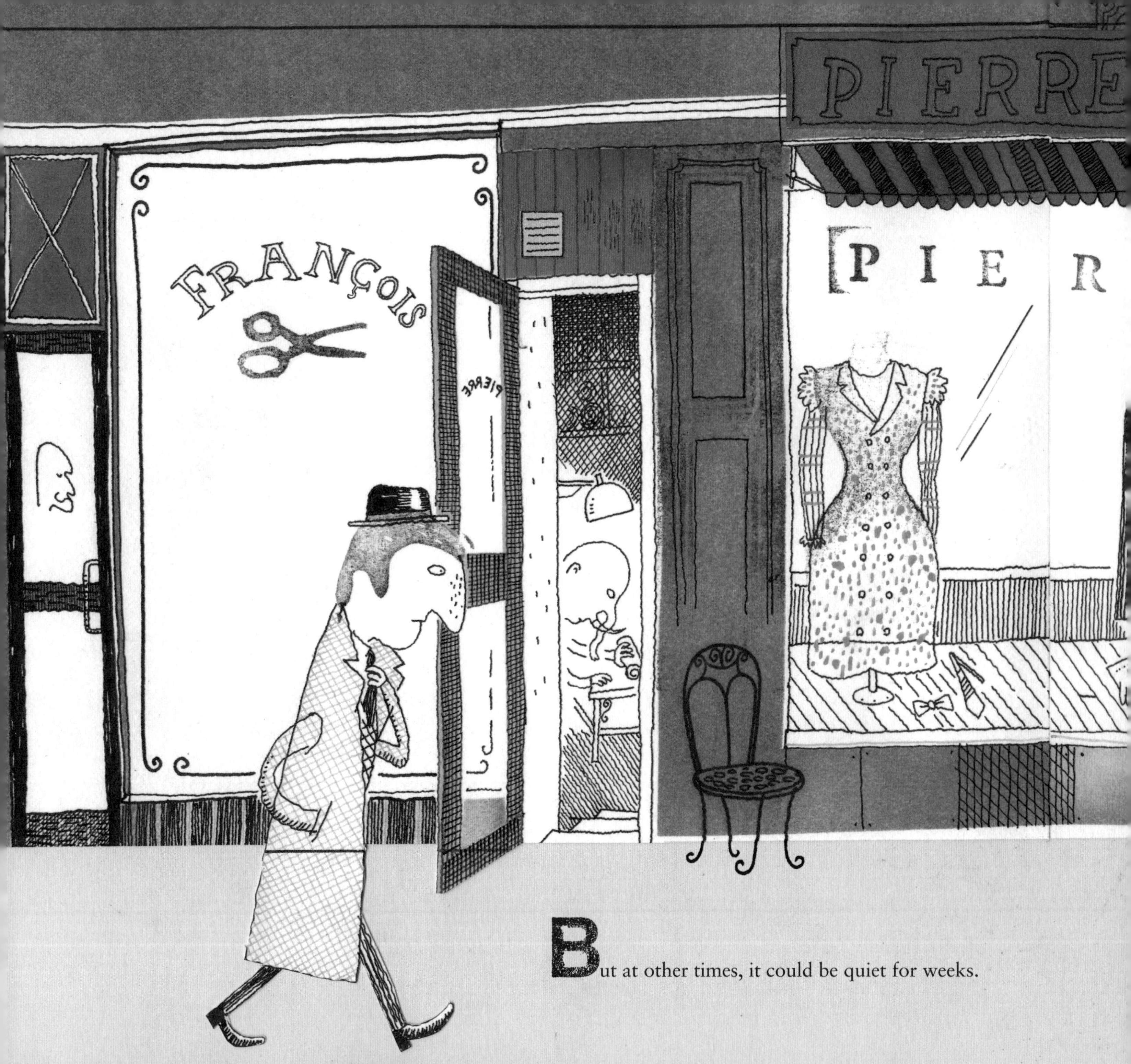
PIERRE
FRANÇOIS
PIERRE
PIE R

But at other times, it could be quiet for weeks.

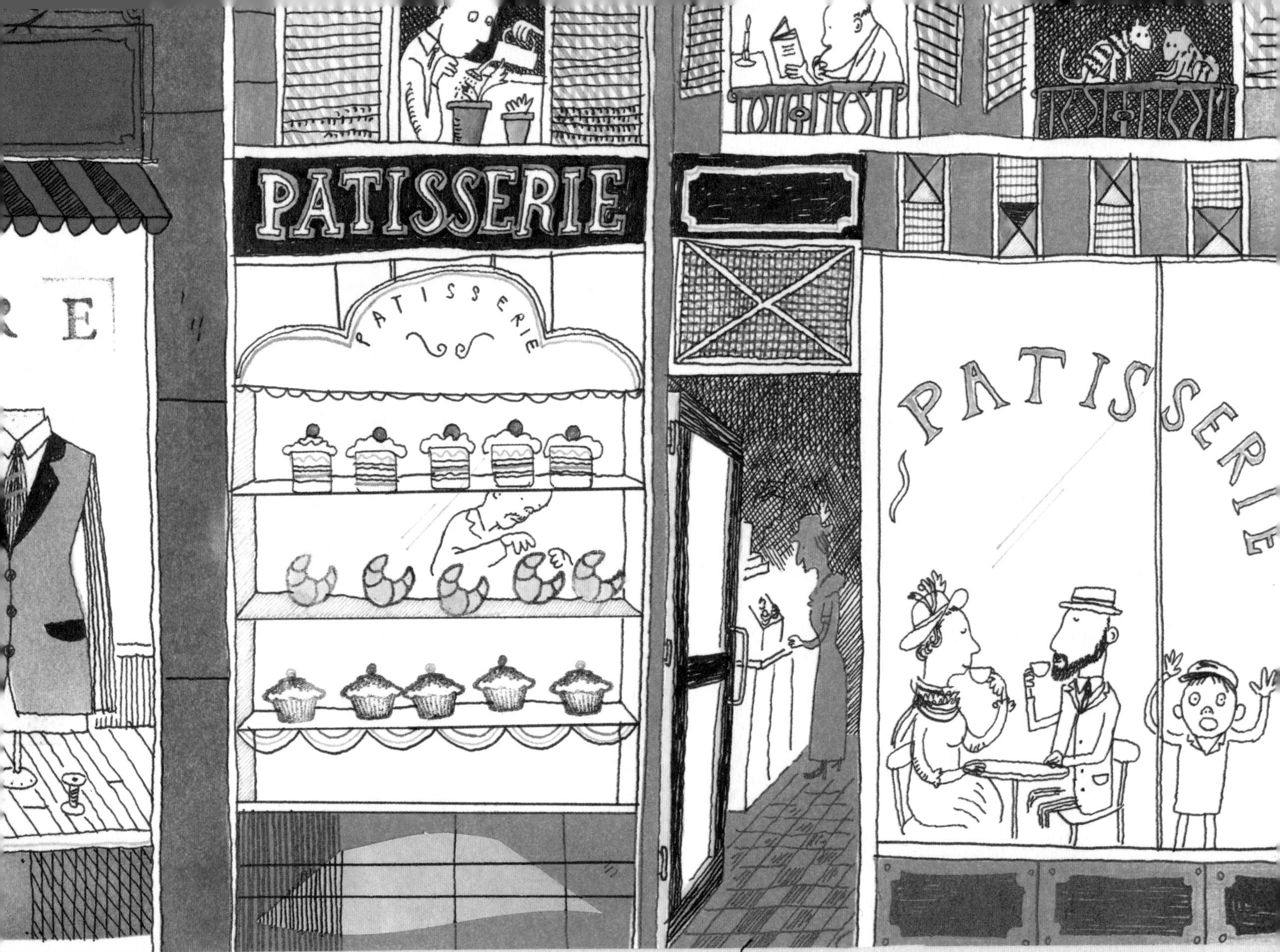
PATISSERIE
PATISSERIE
PATISSERIE
RE

And whenever it was, Pierre sat and thought and daydreamed. You see, he had a very big dream:

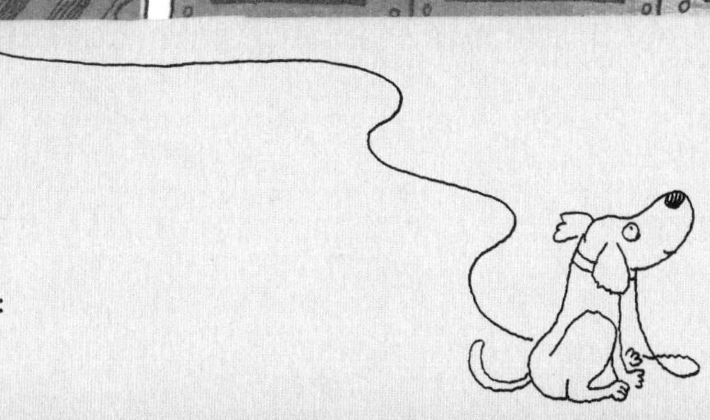

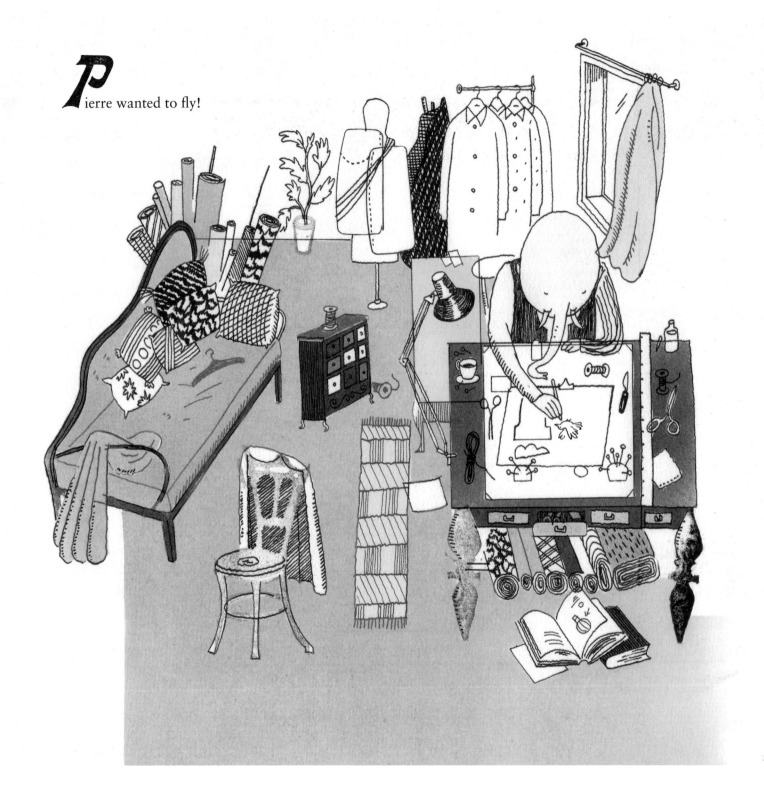

Pierre wanted to fly!

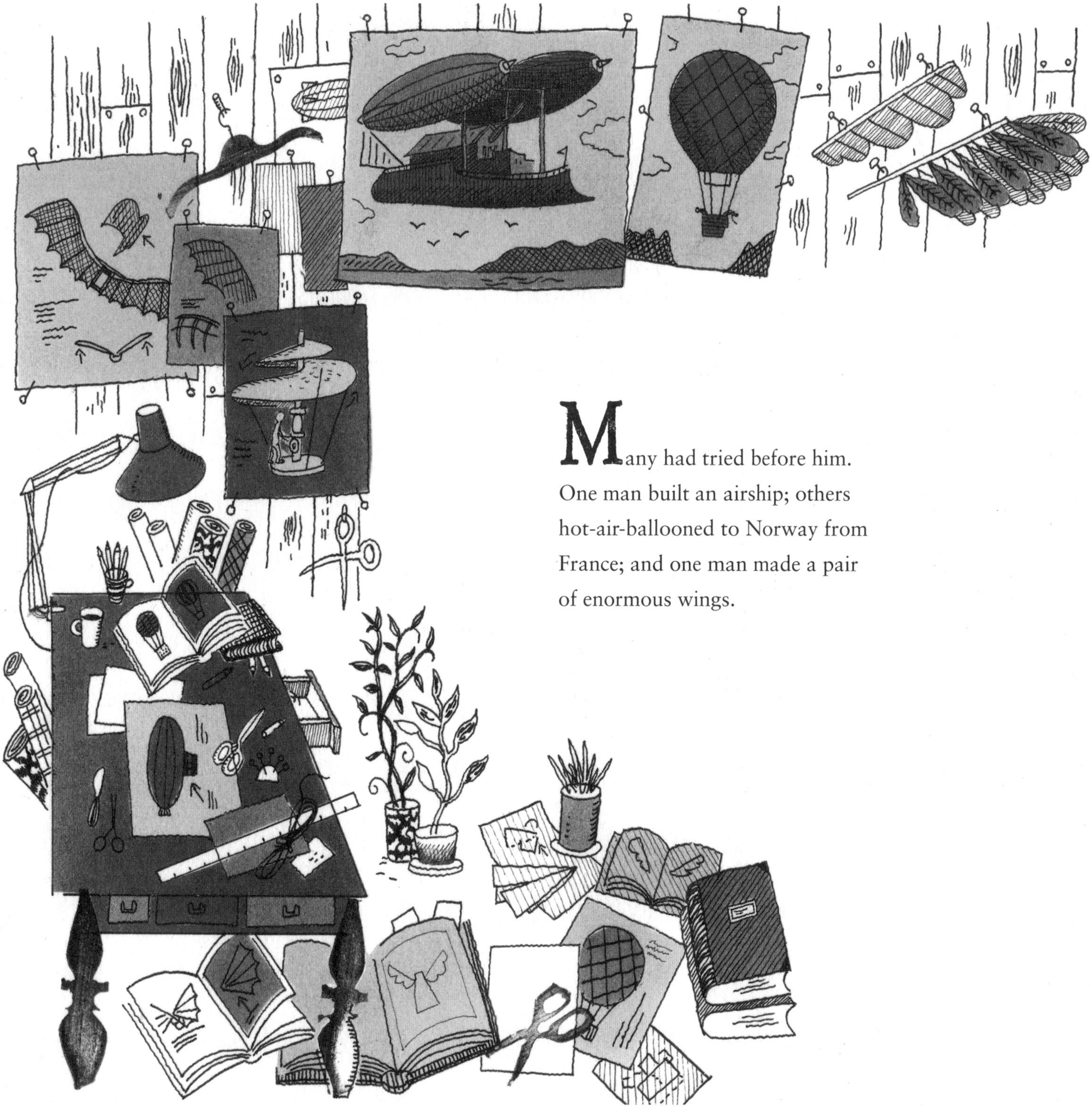

Many had tried before him. One man built an airship; others hot-air-ballooned to Norway from France; and one man made a pair of enormous wings.

No one had ever succeeded,
because flying is a difficult art.
And back in those days,
they didn't know how to do it.

But no one had ever tried
to be a bird!

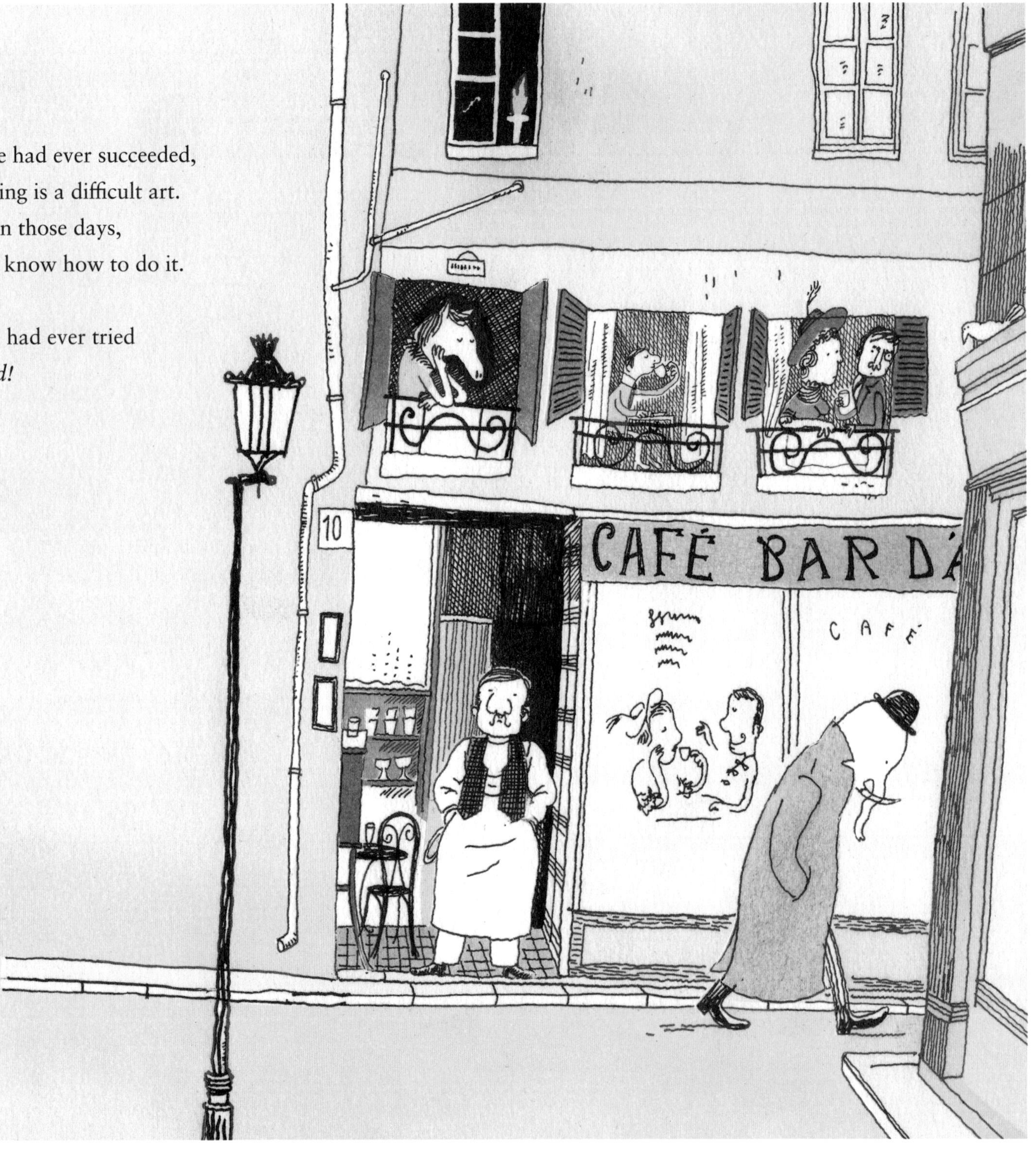
10
CAFÉ BAR D'A
CAFÉ

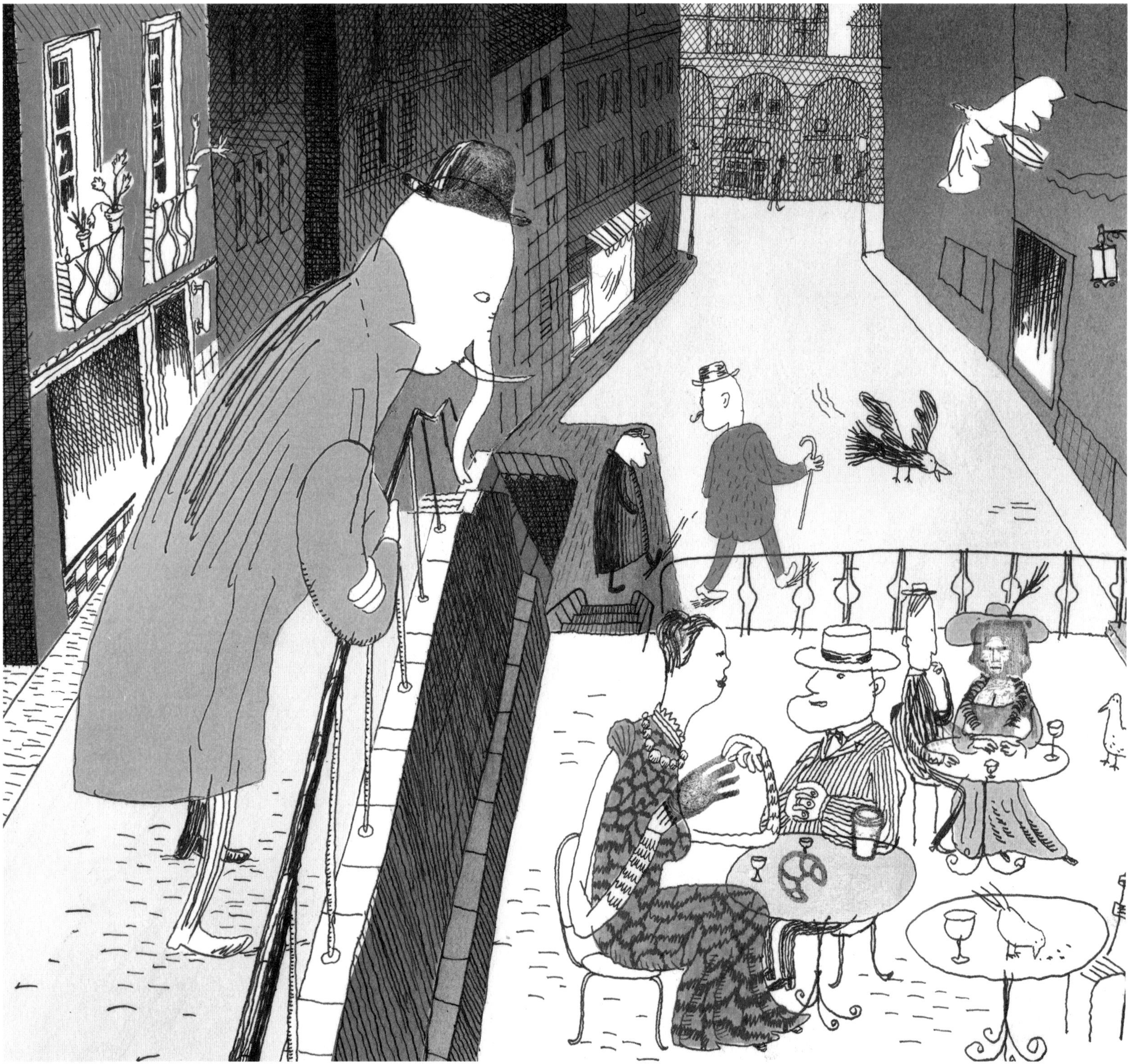

*P*ierre thought that perhaps he was the chosen one. That he, a Parisian tailor, would fly as the first human bird.

"How exciting!" said his neighbor, the barber. "So exciting!

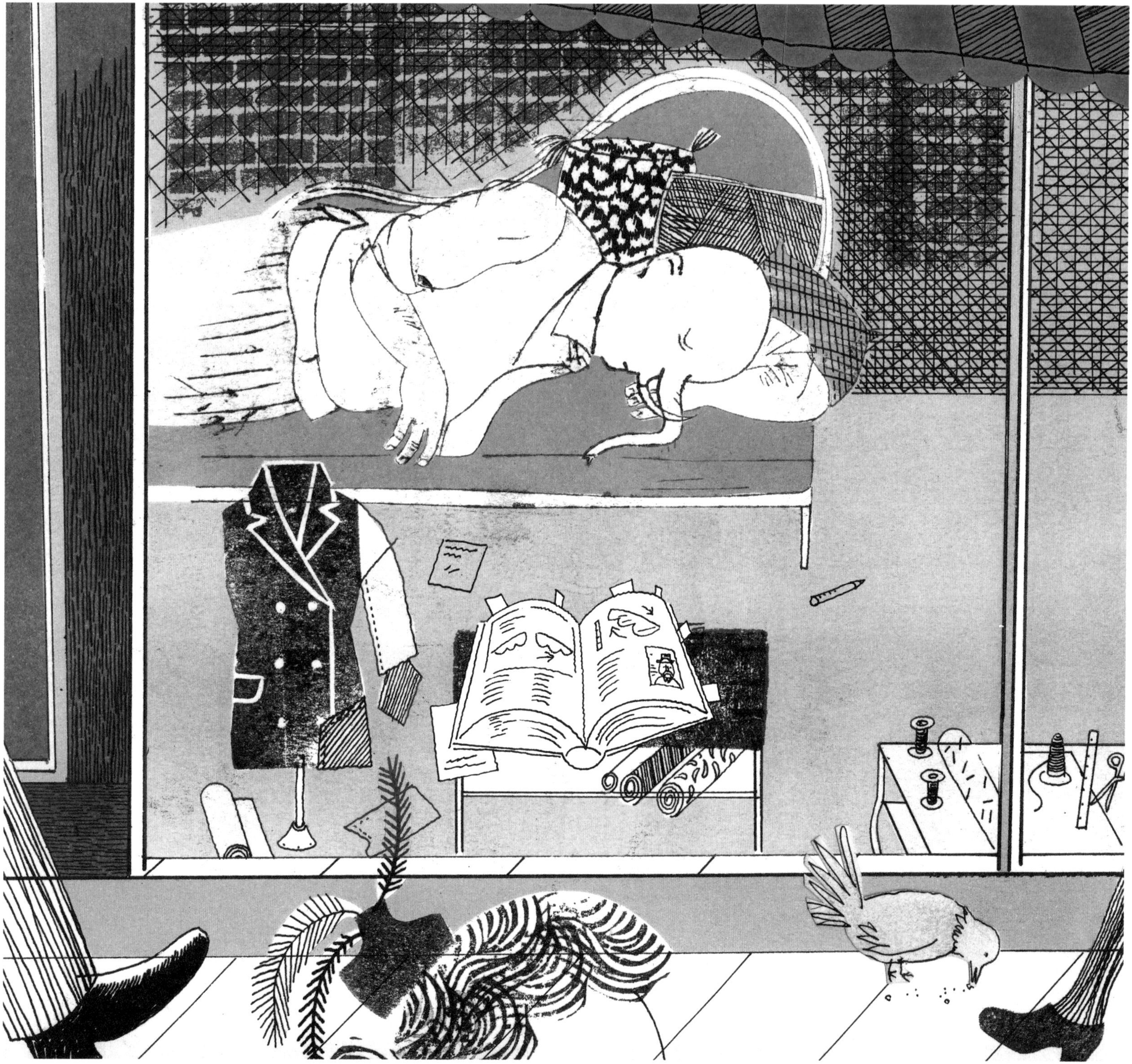

Pierre often thought about becoming a bird.
More and more often, in fact.

He thought about it so often
that one day he closed up his shop
when there was a long line outside.
He didn't have time for tailoring.
His dream was far more important.

So he shuttered the windows
and set to work.

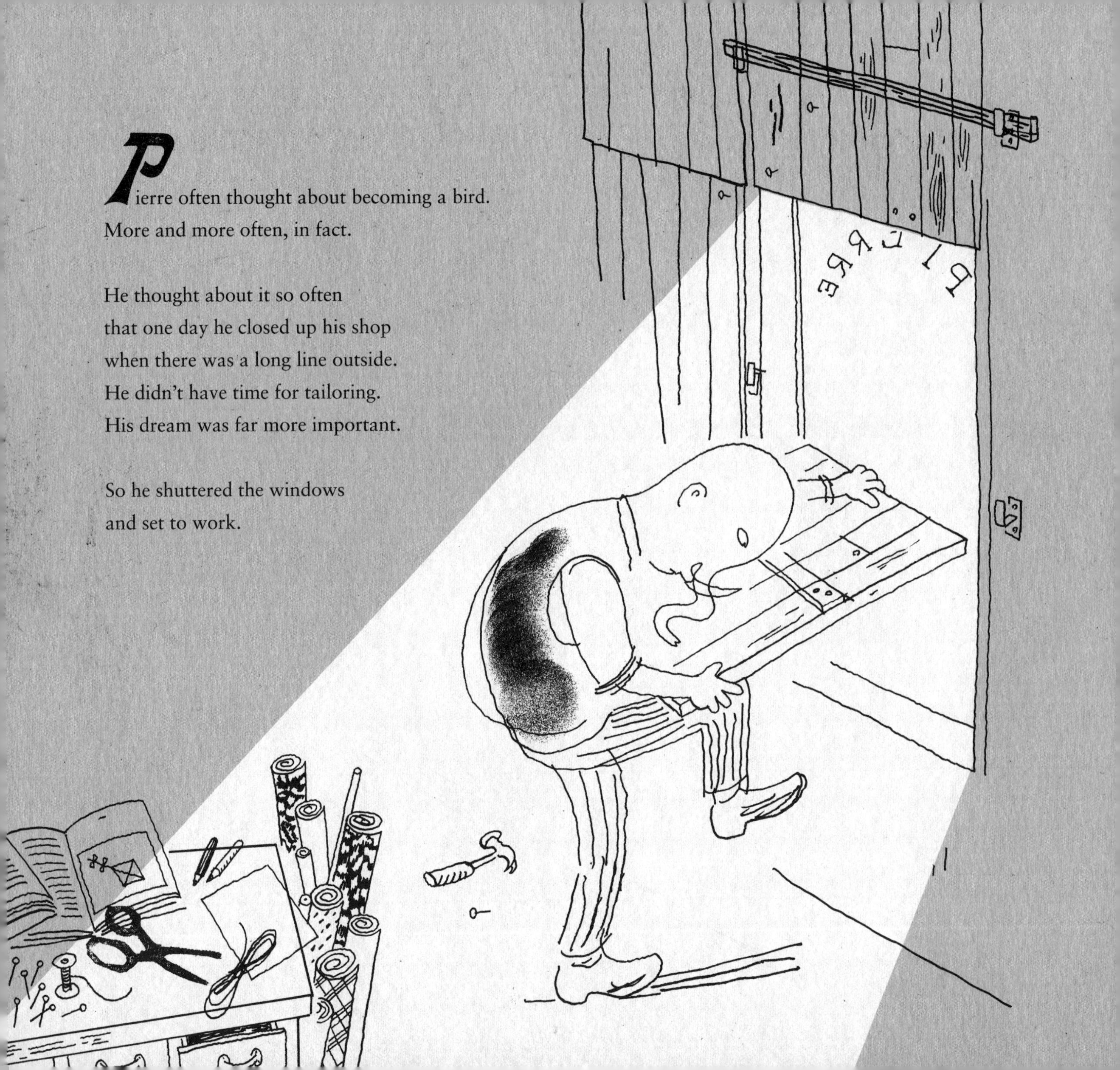

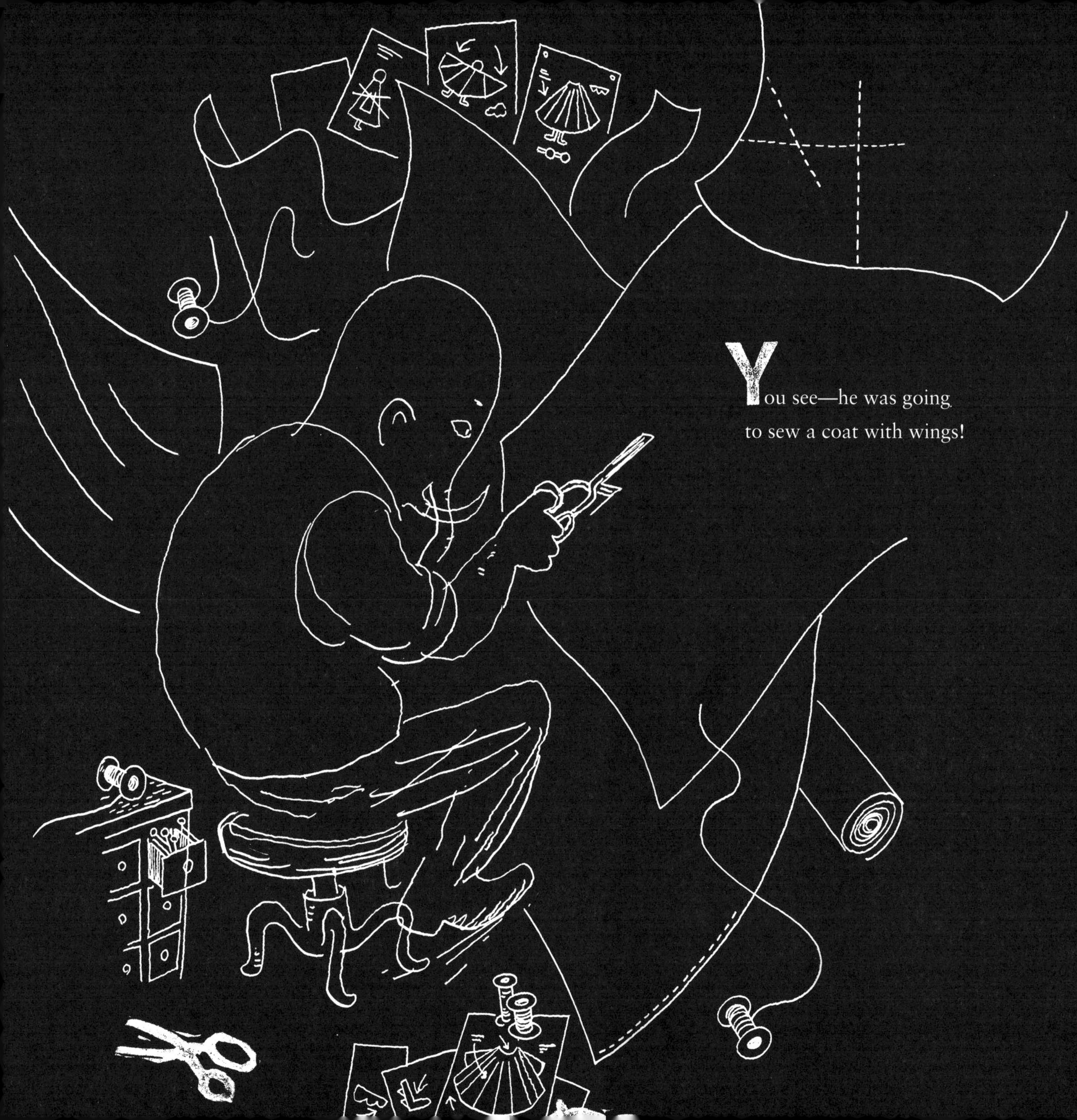

You see—he was going to sew a coat with wings!

And when he put it on, he would be a bird!

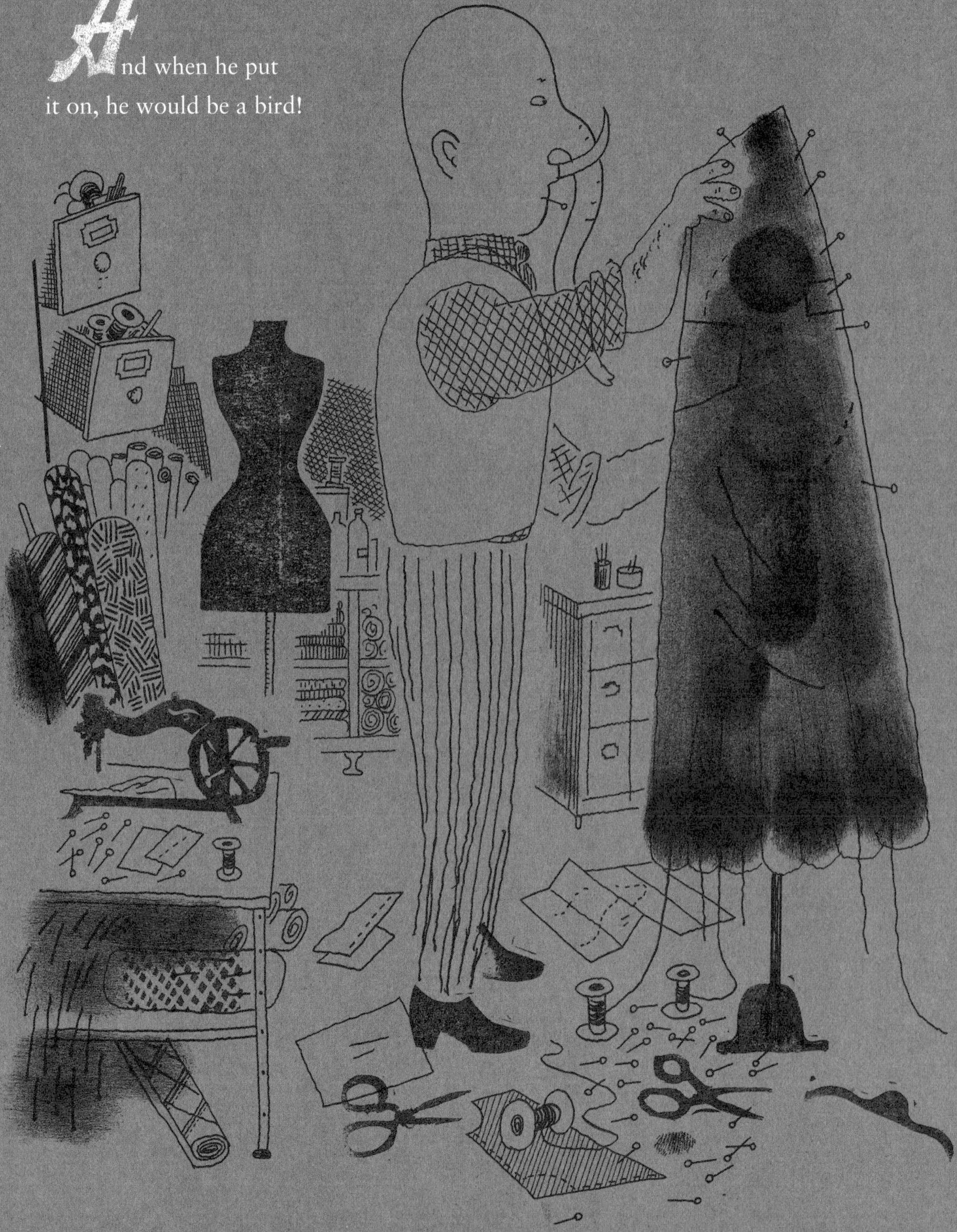

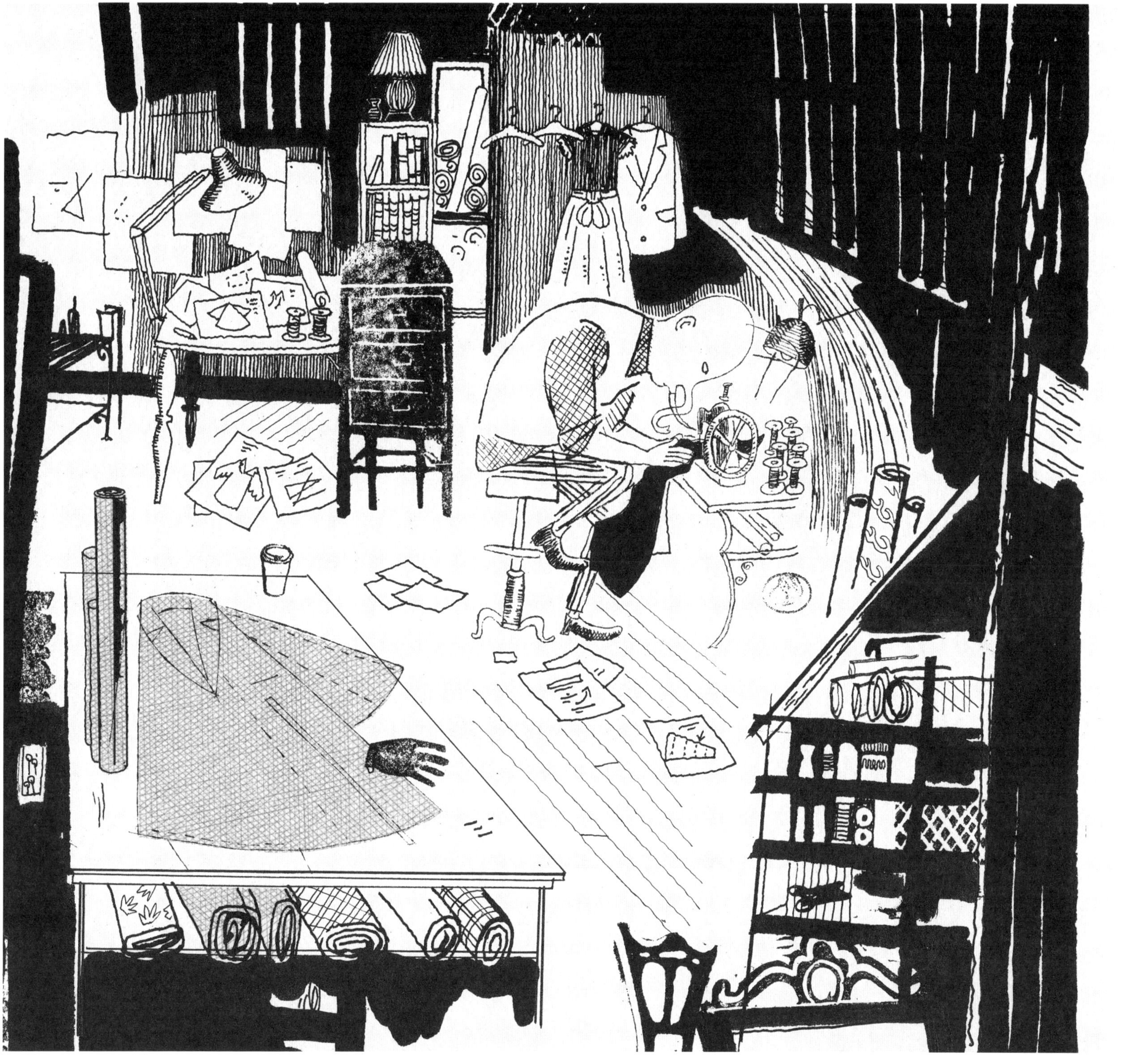

In the evenings, he would stand in front of the mirror and admire his handiwork. "Excellent, Pierre, excellent," he would say.

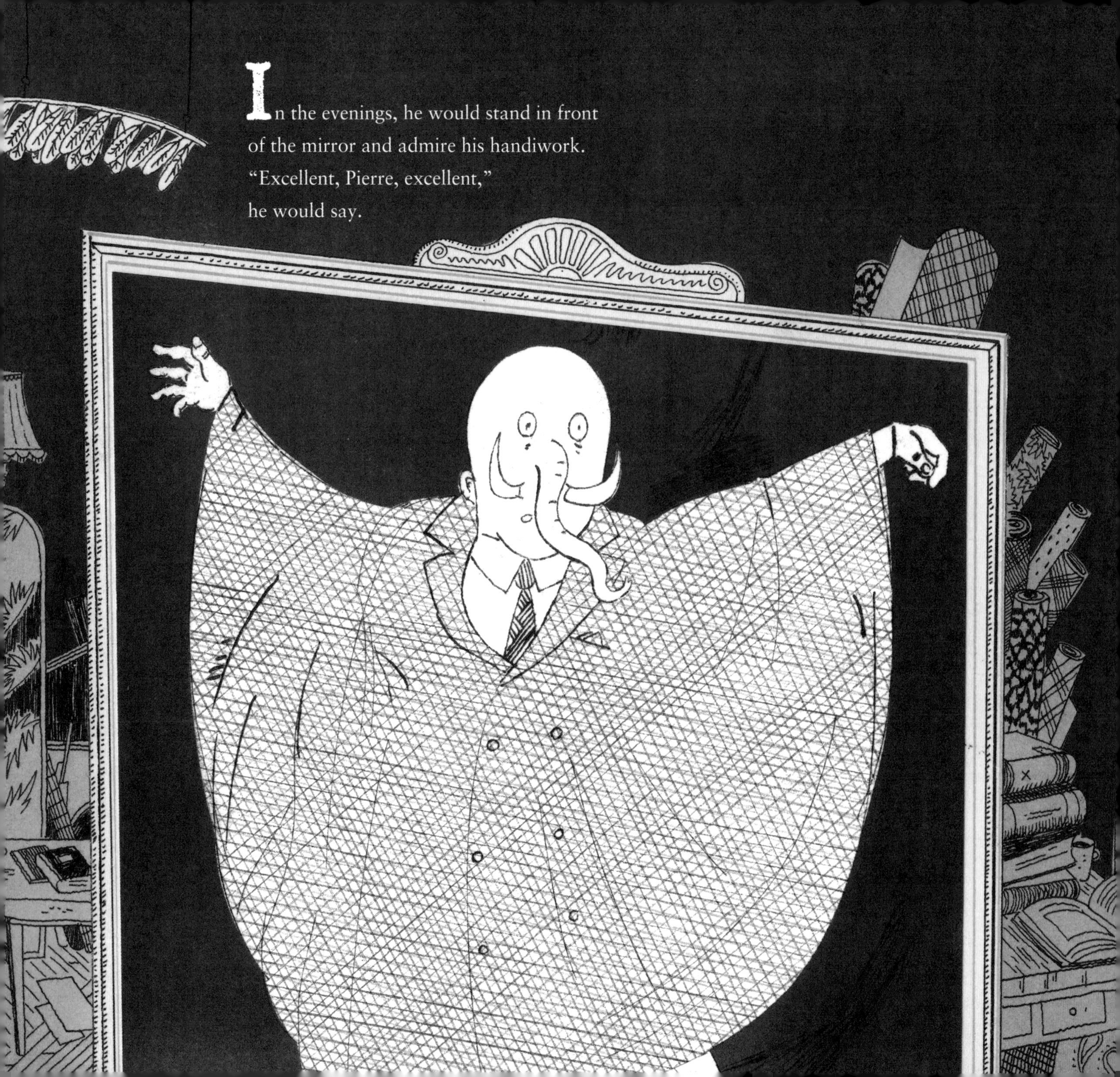

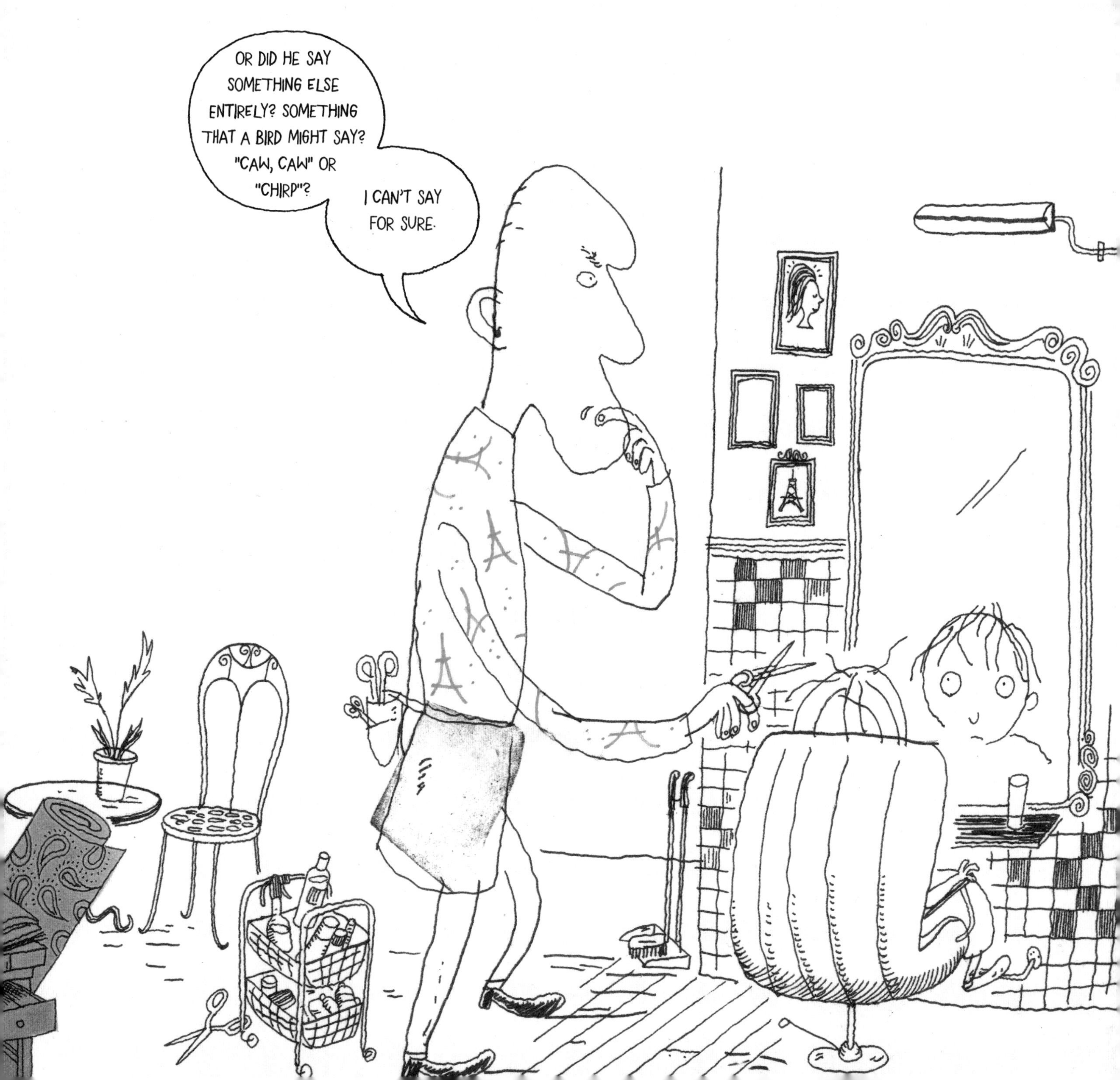
OR DID HE SAY SOMETHING ELSE ENTIRELY? SOMETHING THAT A BIRD MIGHT SAY? "CAW, CAW" OR "CHIRP"?
I CAN'T SAY FOR SURE.

When the coat was ready,
he called all the newspapers.

"Tomorrow, Saturday, I,
Pierre the tailor, will fly
from the Eiffel Tower,"
he told the first and the second
and the third newspaper.

To the last, so there would be
no doubt as to what was going
to happen and who he was, he said:
"Tomorrow, I, Pierre the bird,
will fly from the Eiffel Tower."

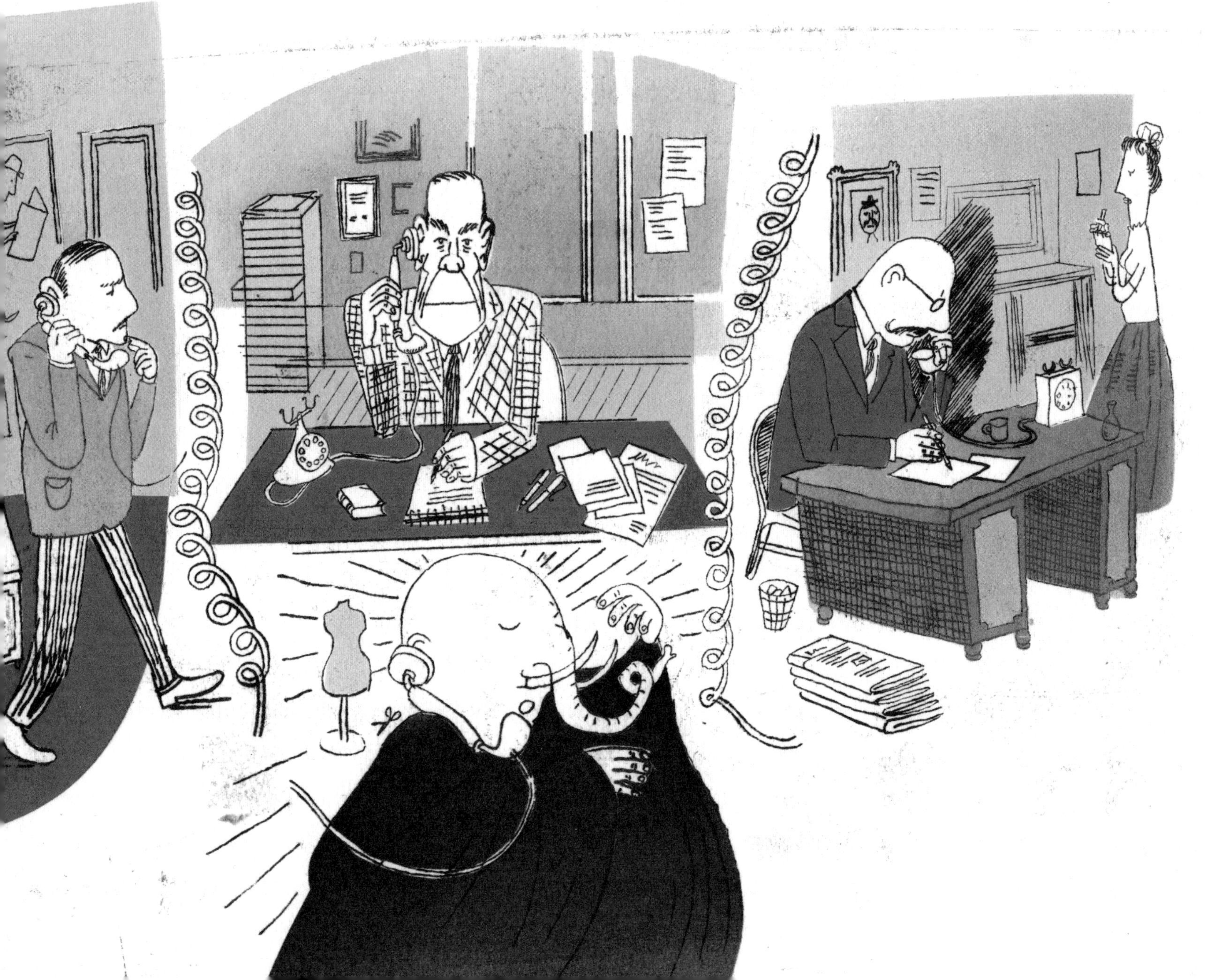

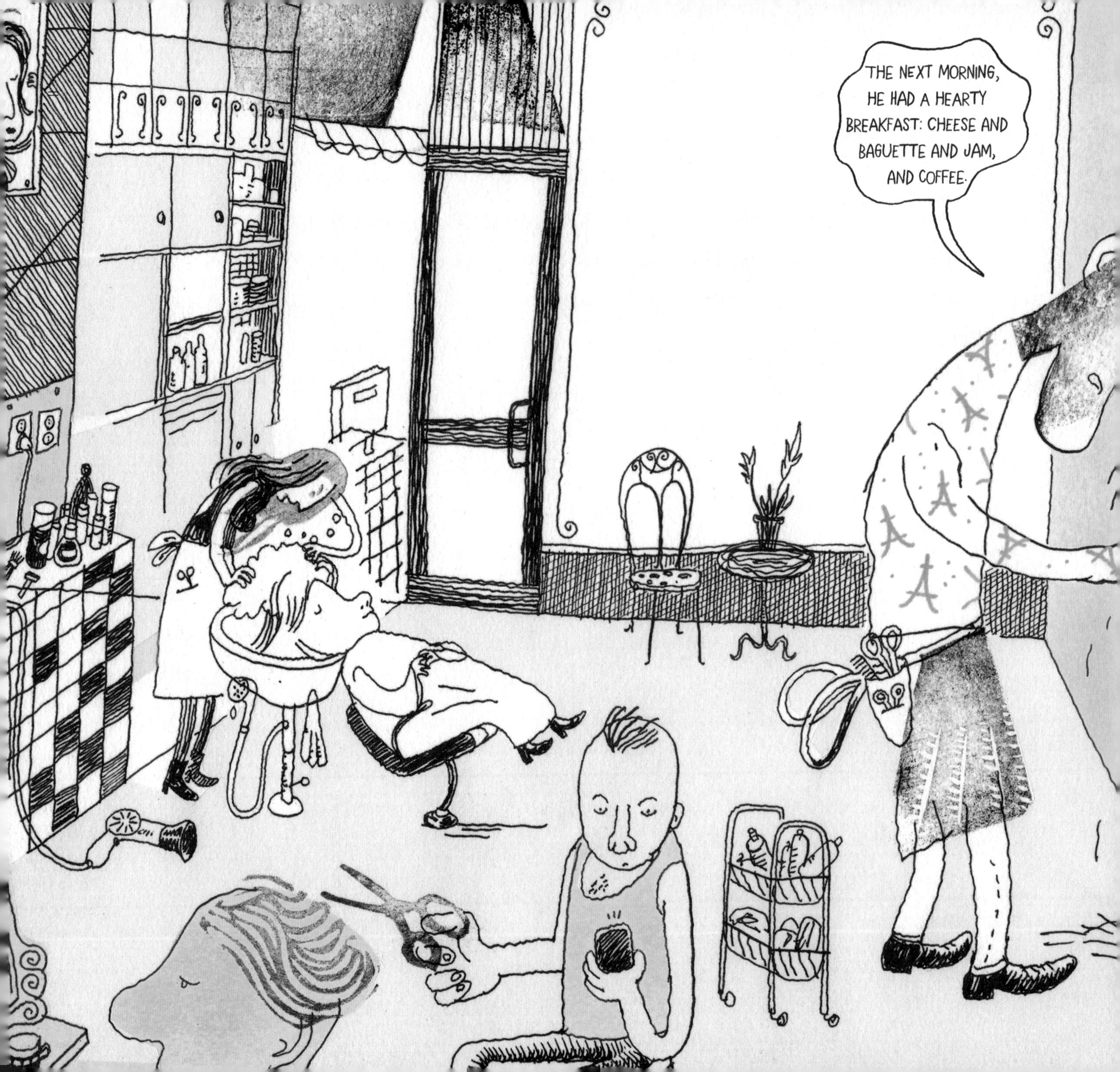
THE NEXT MORNING, HE HAD A HEARTY BREAKFAST: CHEESE AND BAGUETTE AND JAM, AND COFFEE.

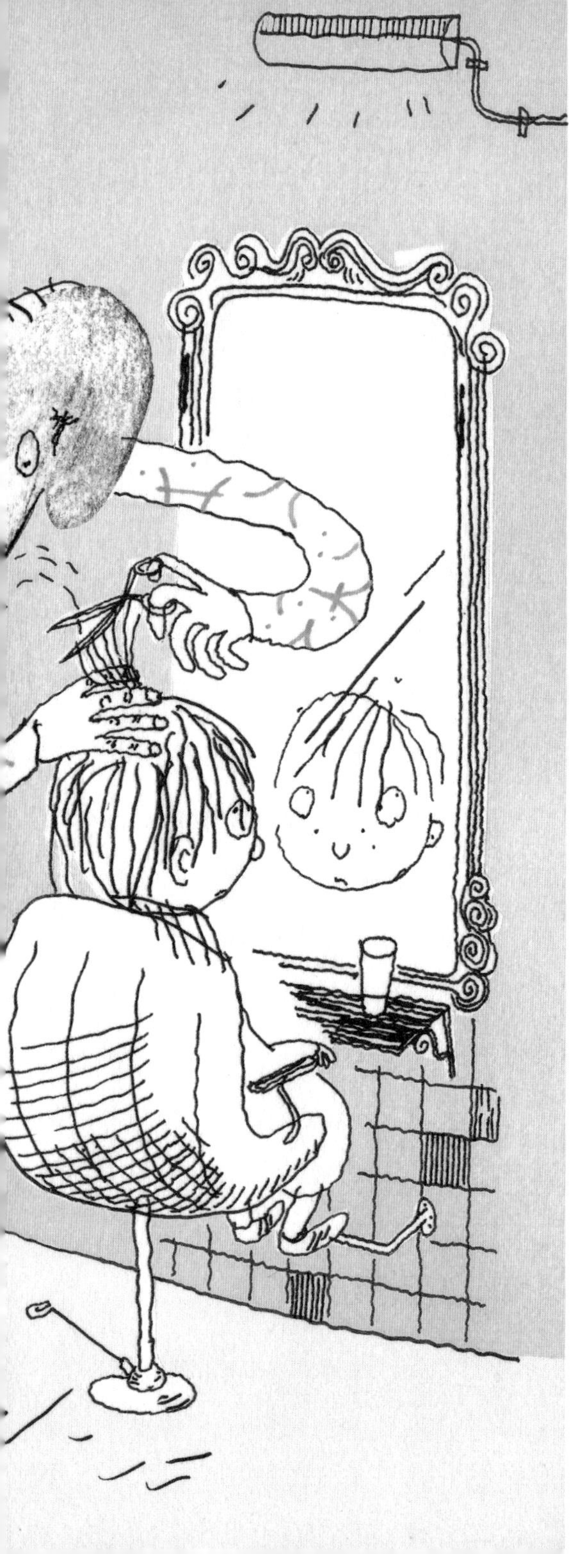

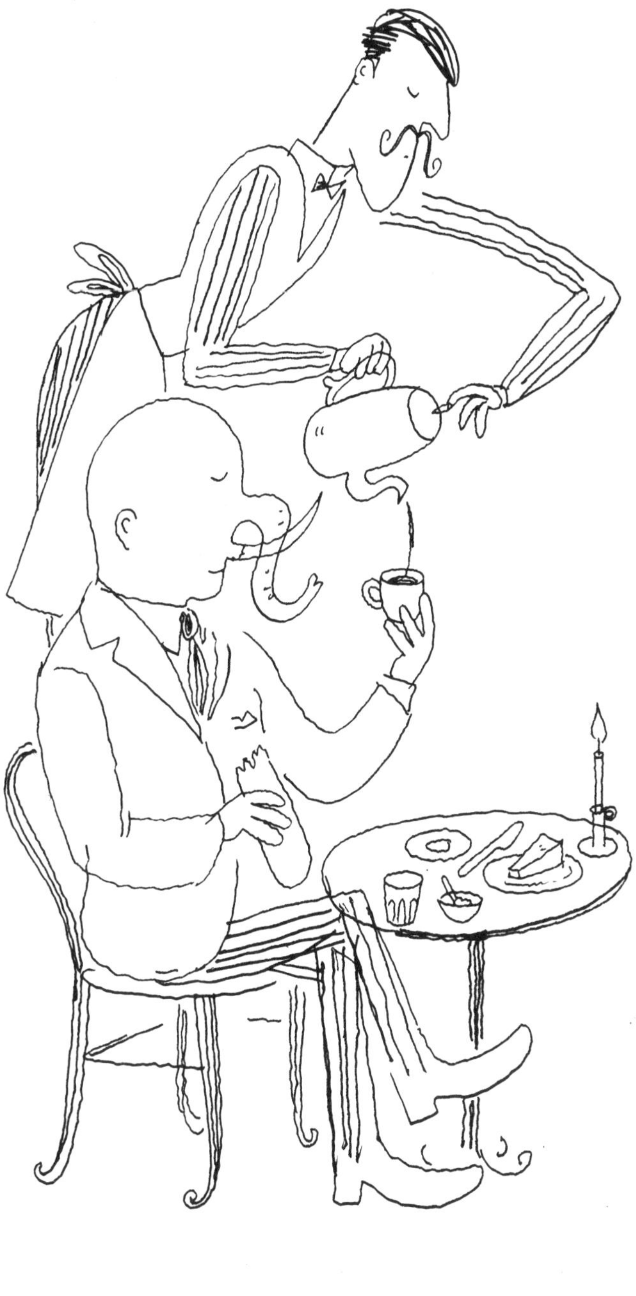

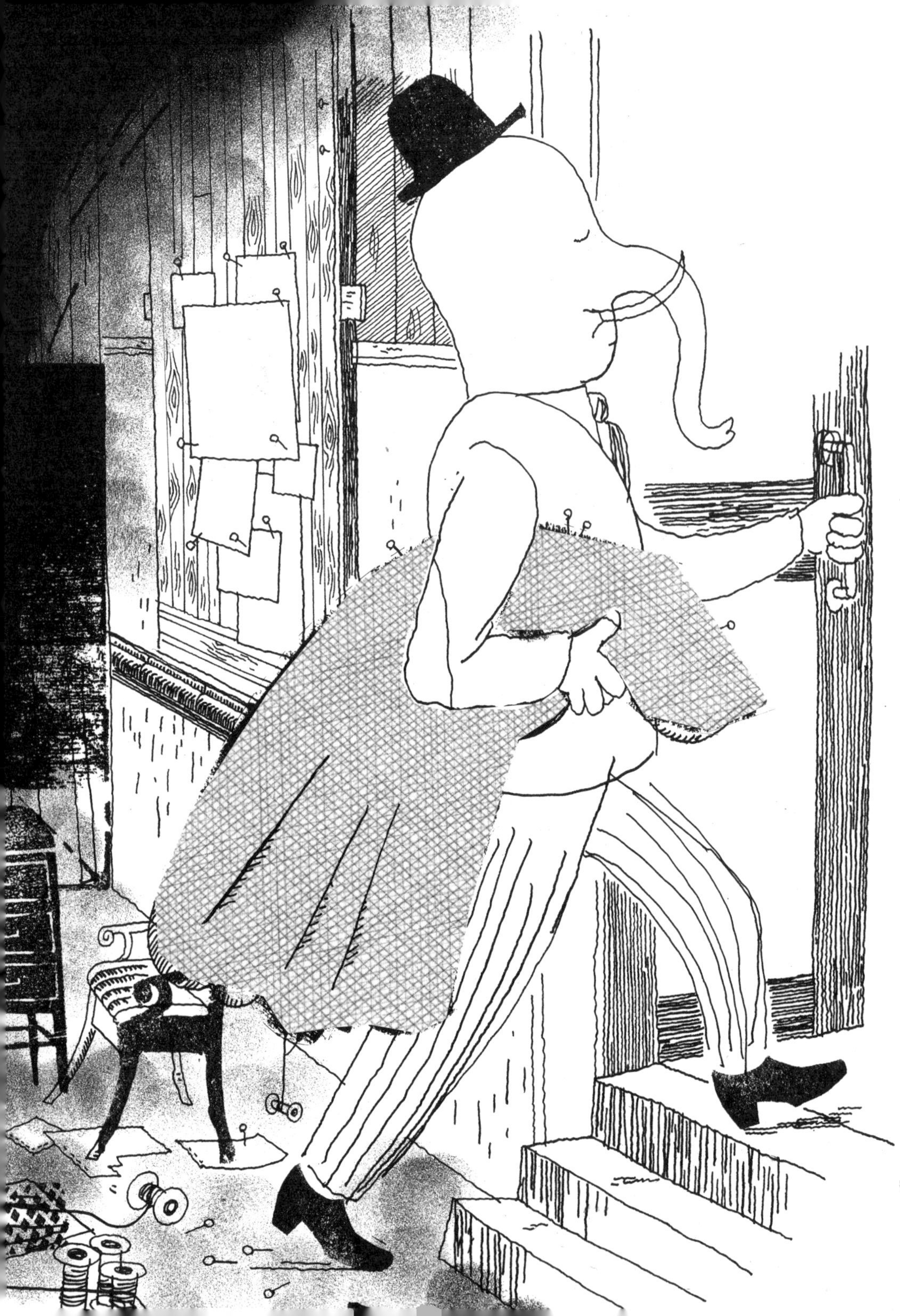

Then off he went, with his bird coat under his arm.

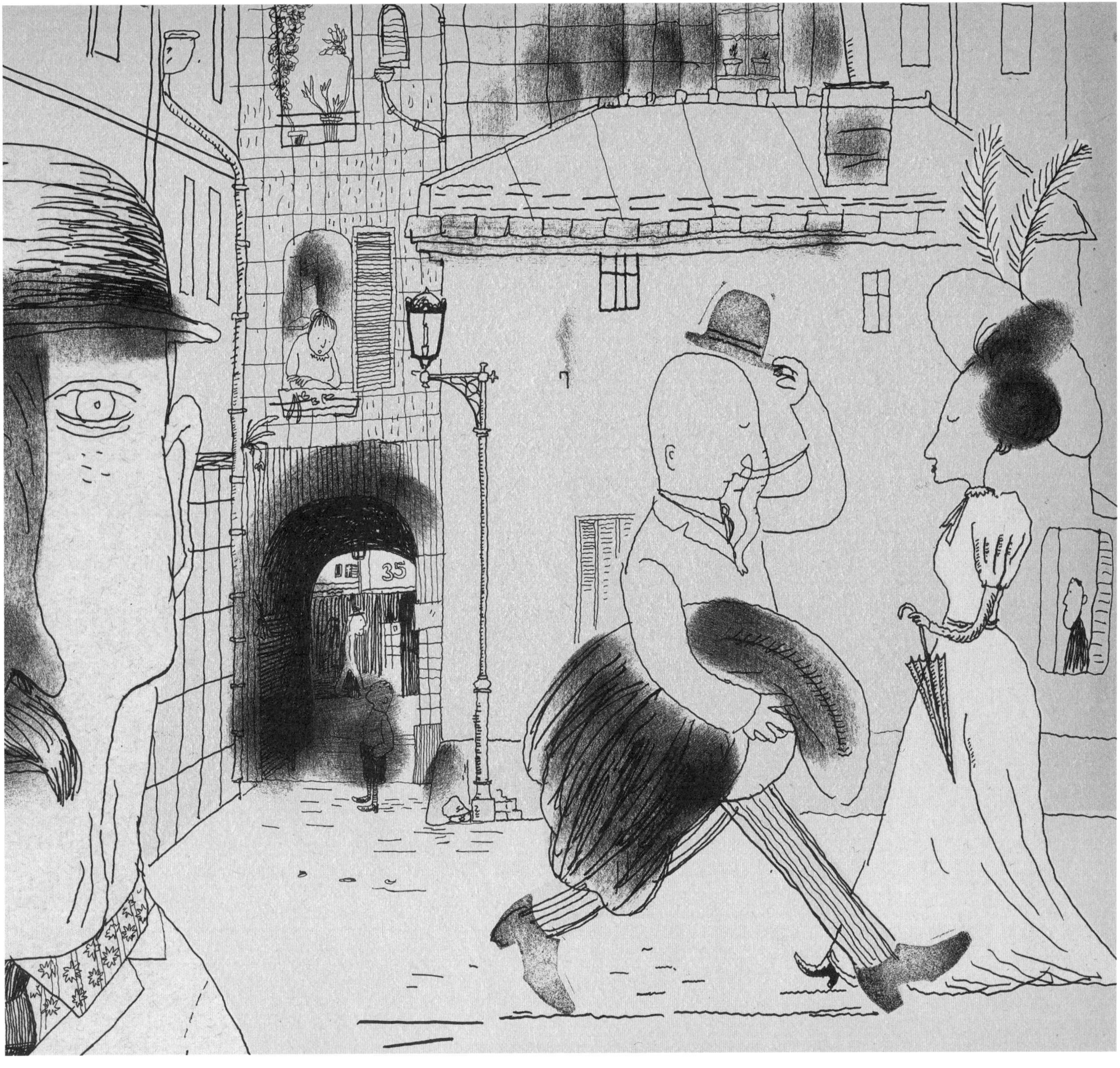
35

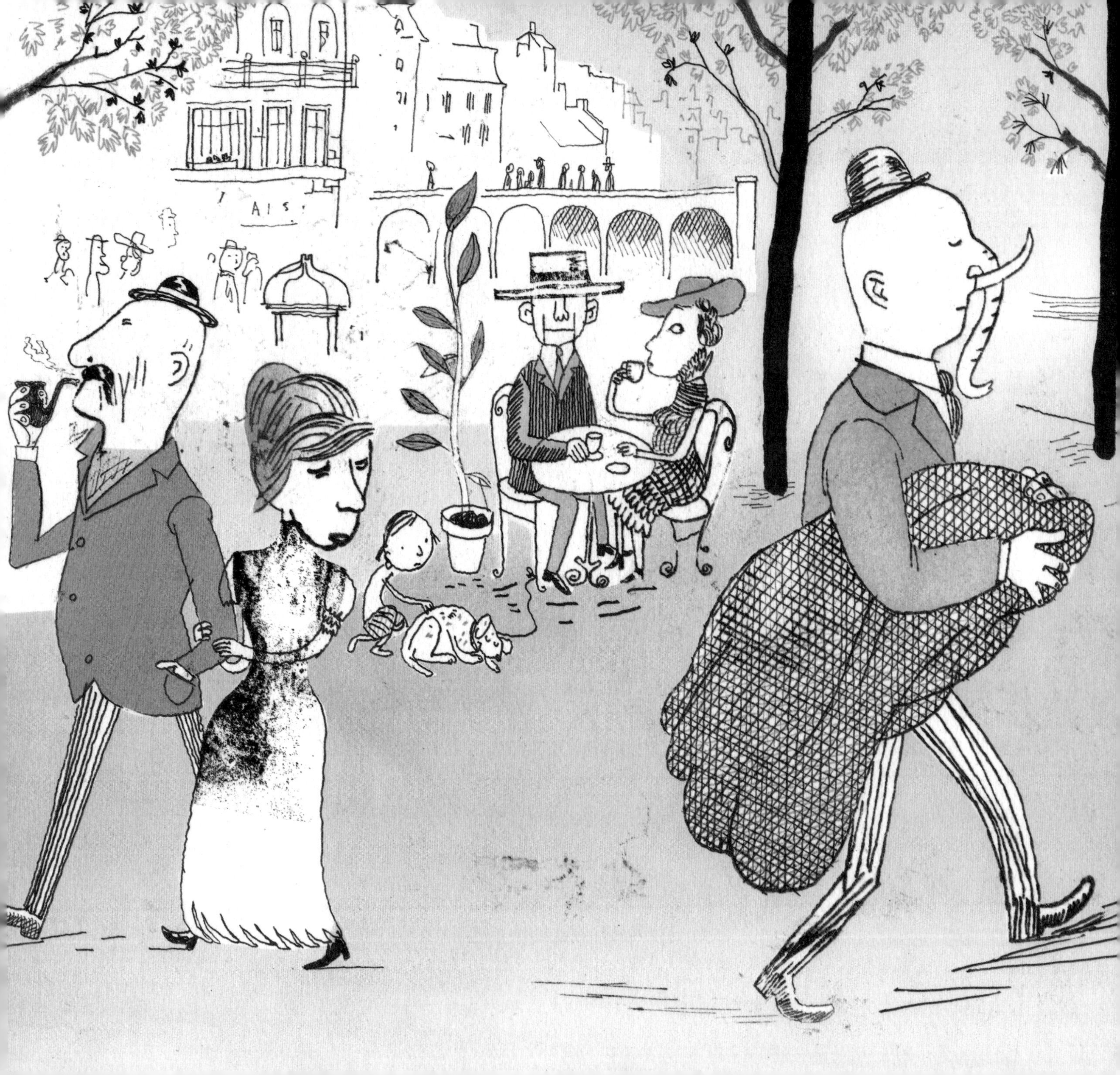

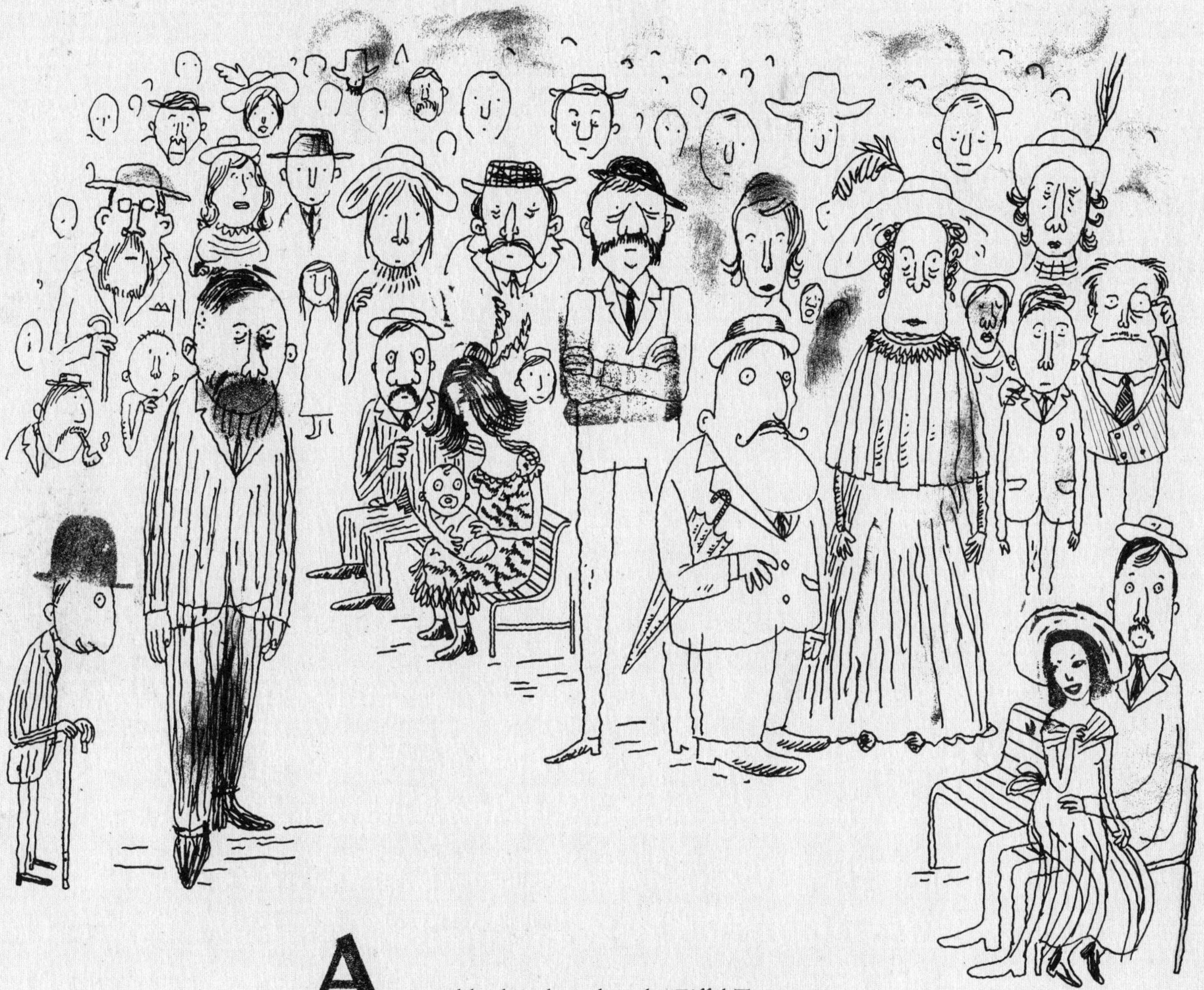

A crowd had gathered at the Eiffel Tower.
All the newspapers and many of his customers were there.

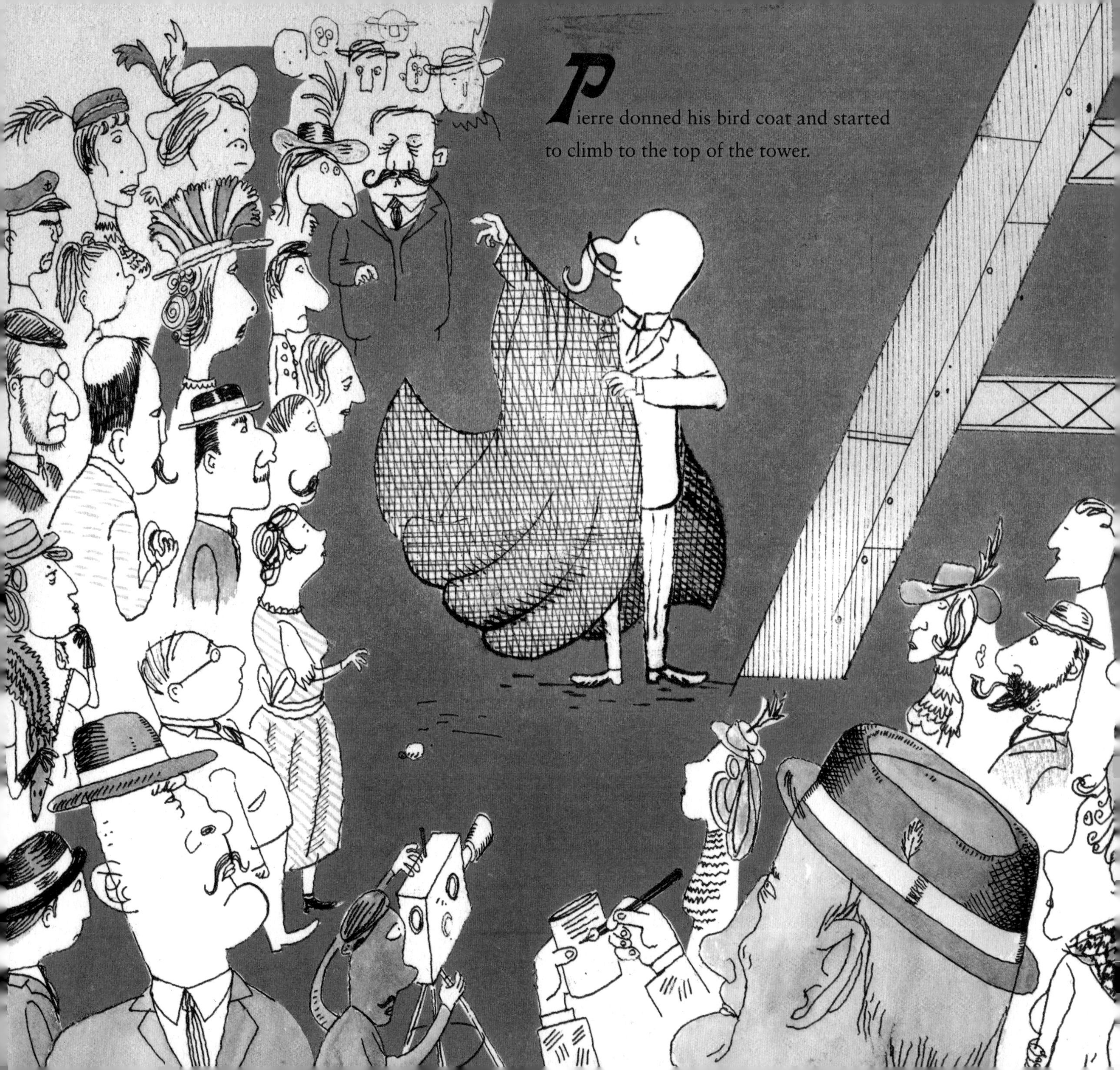

Pierre donned his bird coat and started to climb to the top of the tower.

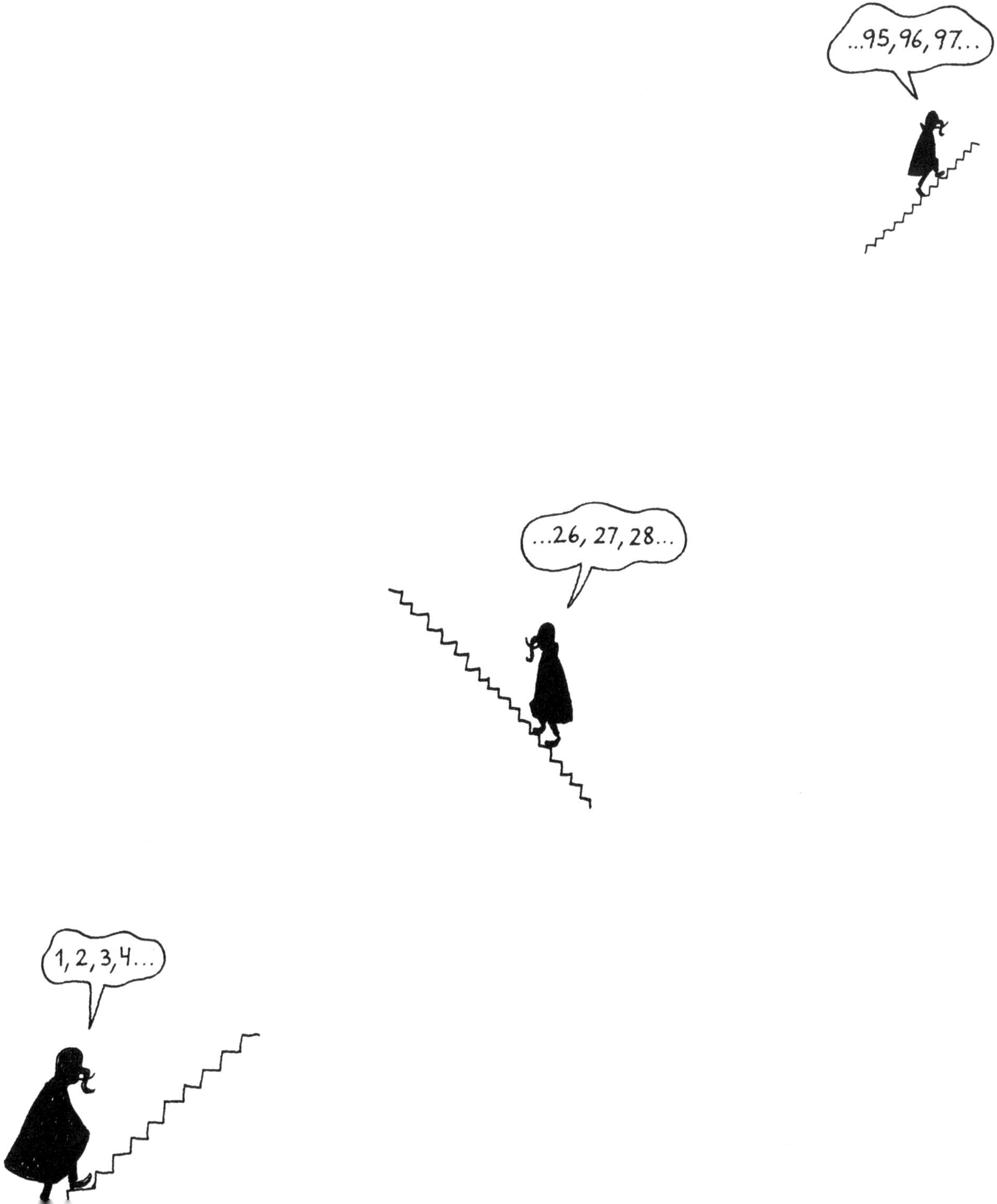
1, 2, 3, 4...
...26, 27, 28...
...95, 96, 97...

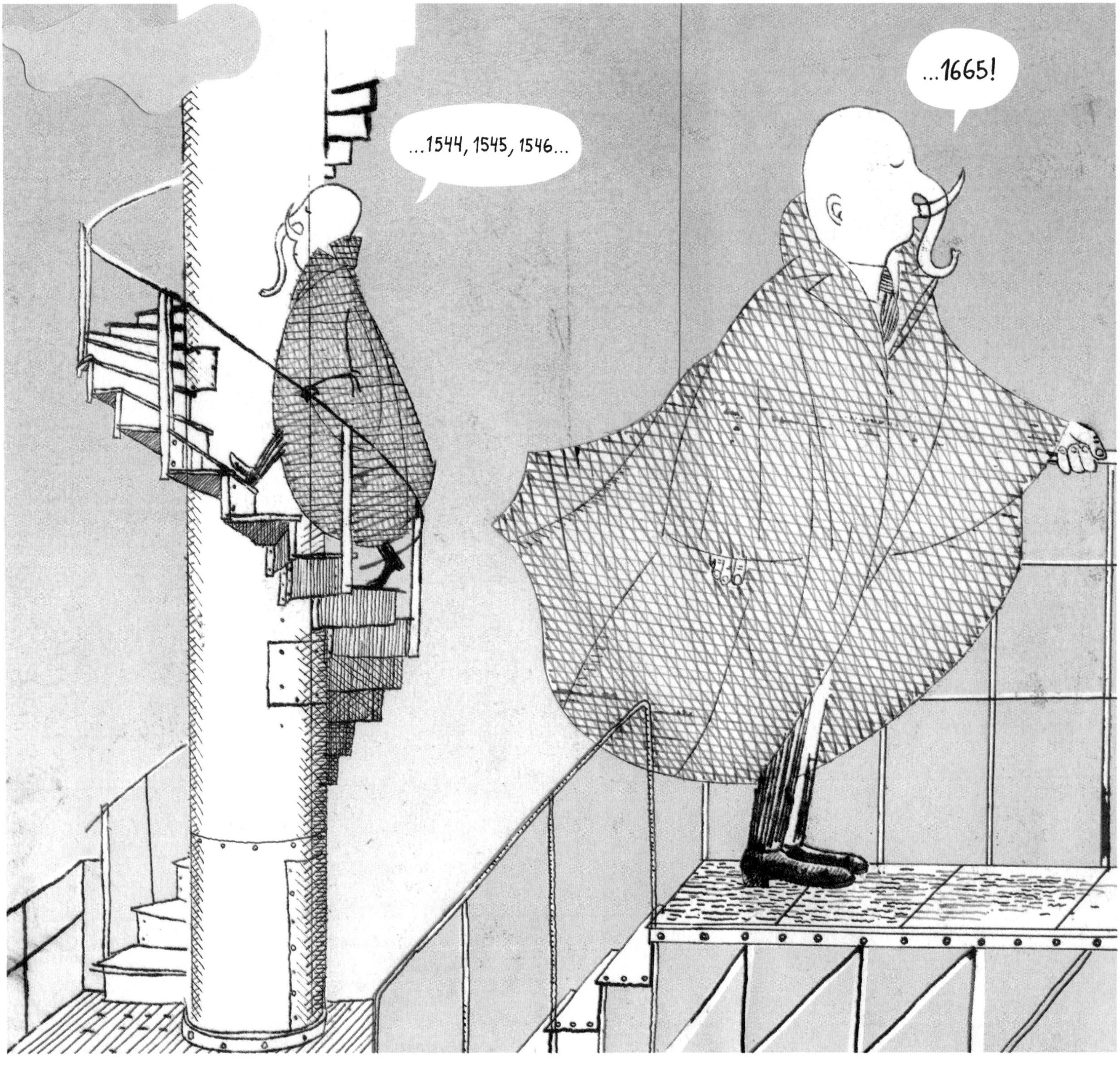
...1544, 1545, 1546...
...1665!

At the top, stood François the barber. The two old friends solemnly shook hands.

"Good luck," said François. "Have a good flight."

"So long, for now," said Pierre, and he gave his friend a hug.

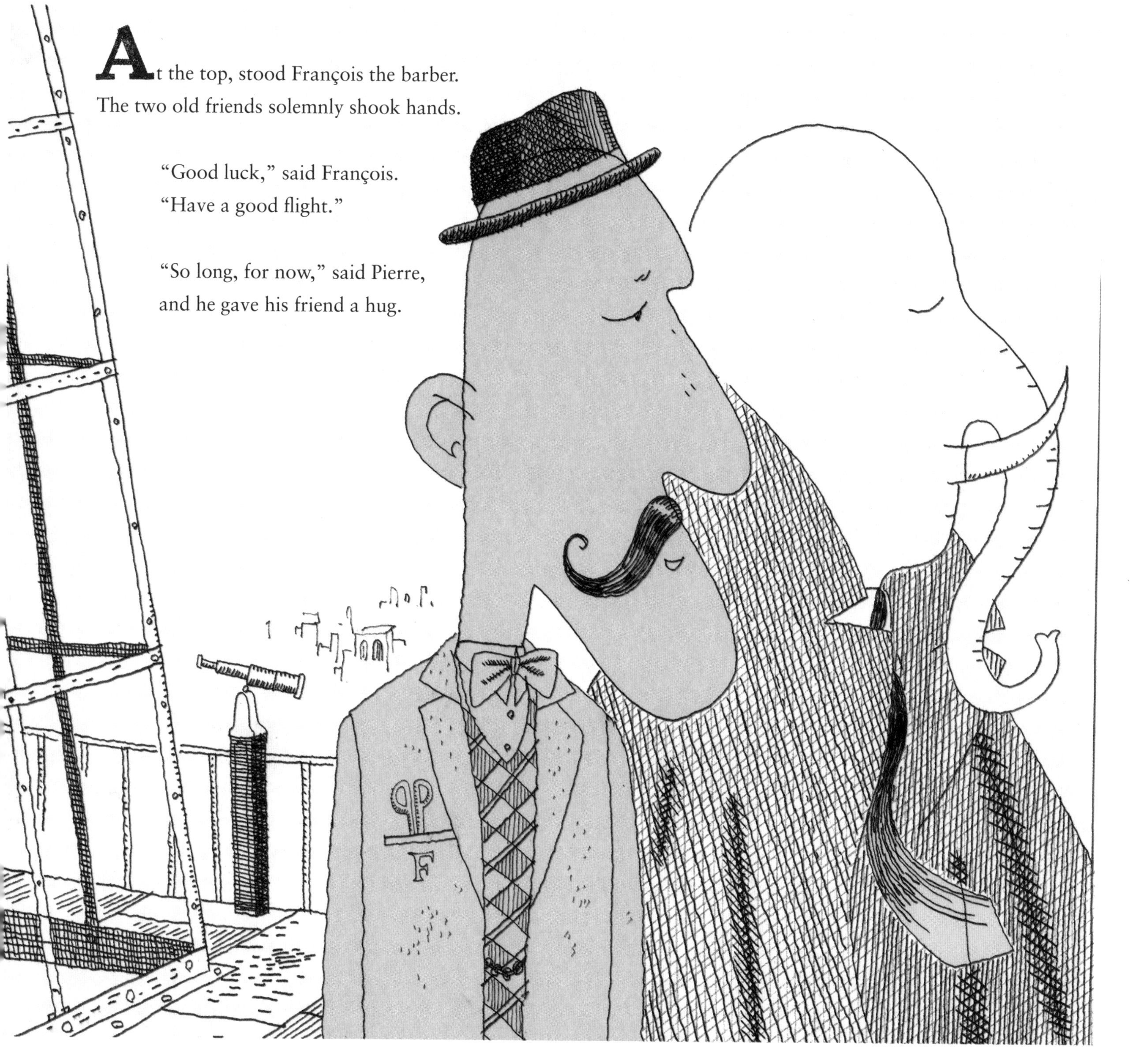

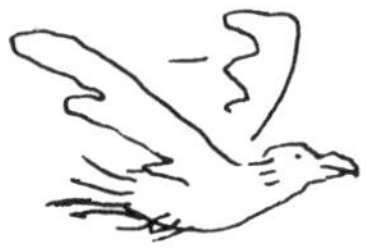

Pierre stood
at the edge,
at the top
of the Eiffel Tower
and looked out
over Paris.

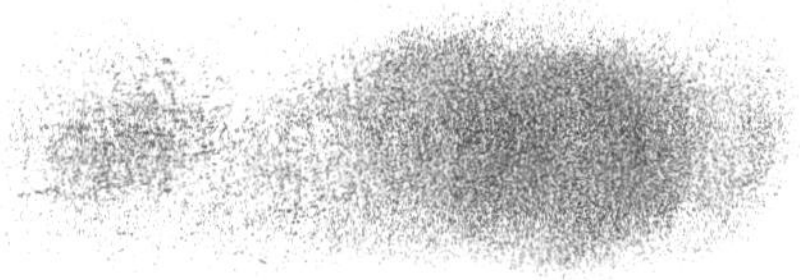

Pierre waited
and waited
and waited
for the right moment.
The clouds drifted slowly by.

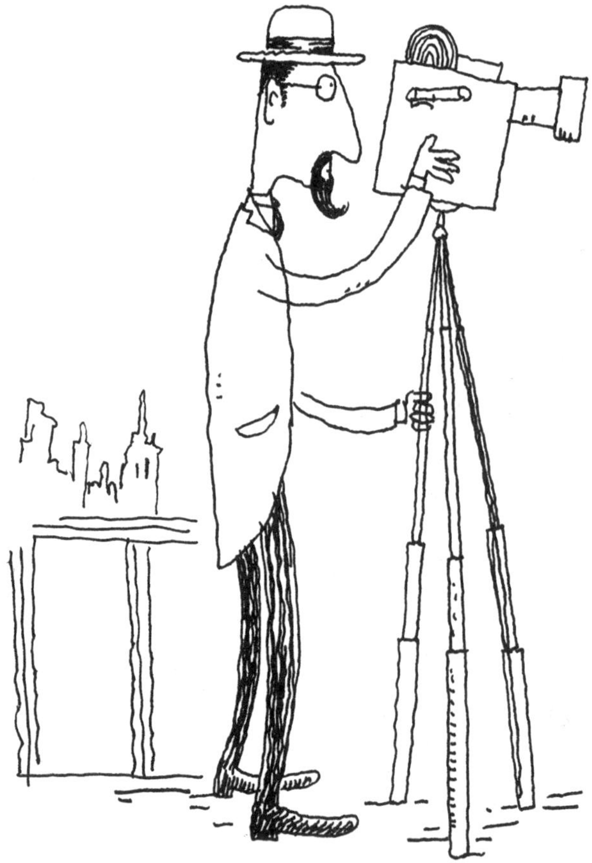

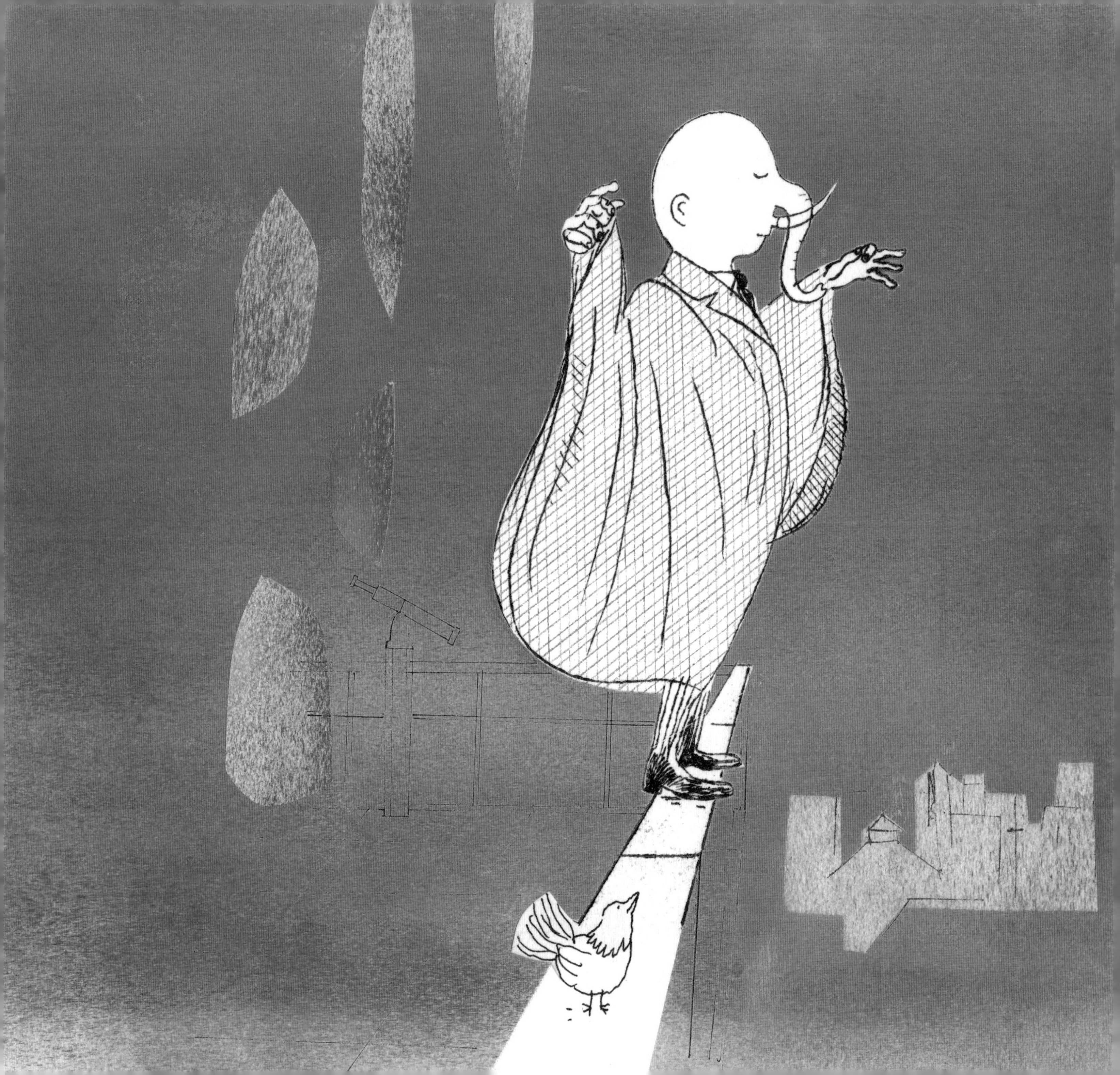

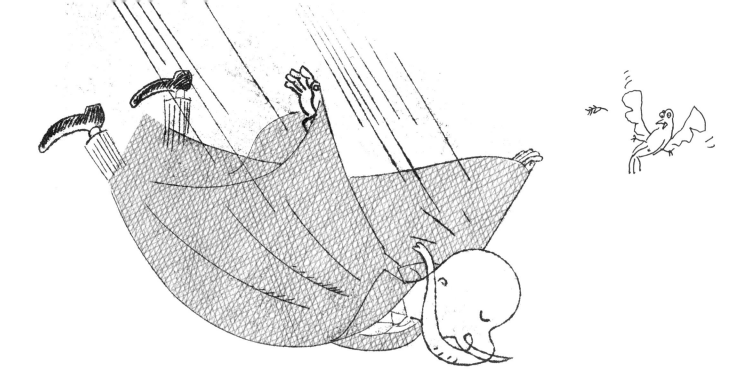

Then Pierre the bird jumped.

One or two real birds sailed past him
and twittered at his woolen coat as it
fluttered. Pierre flapped his wings.
He really was trying to fly.

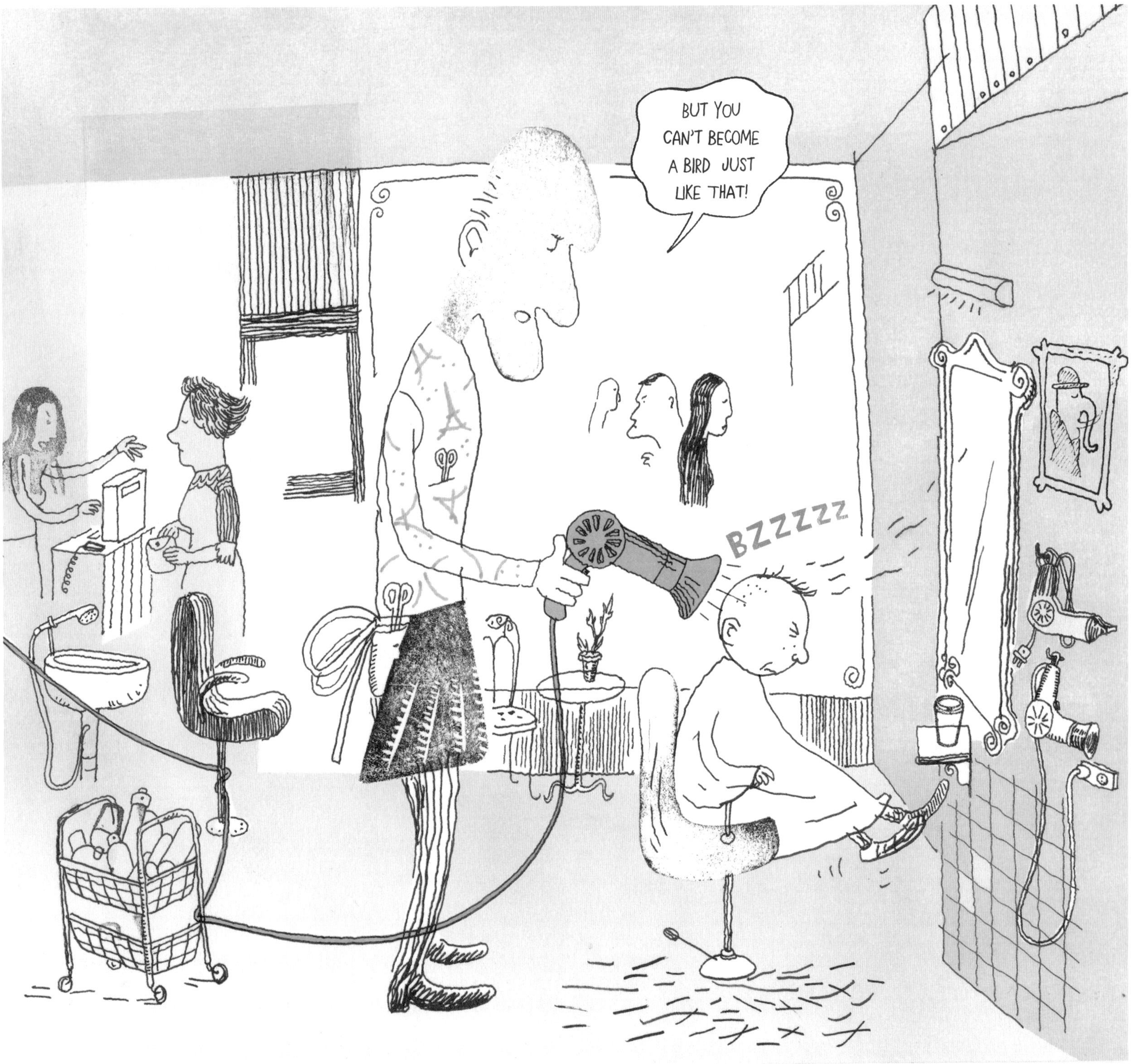
BUT YOU CAN'T BECOME A BIRD JUST LIKE THAT!
BZZZZZ

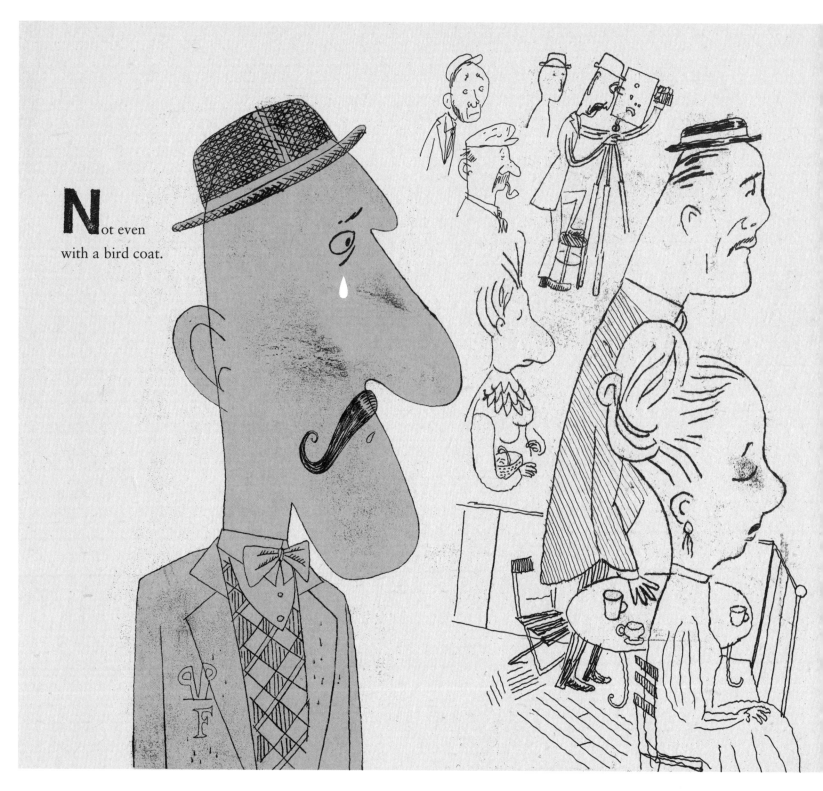

Not even
with a bird coat.

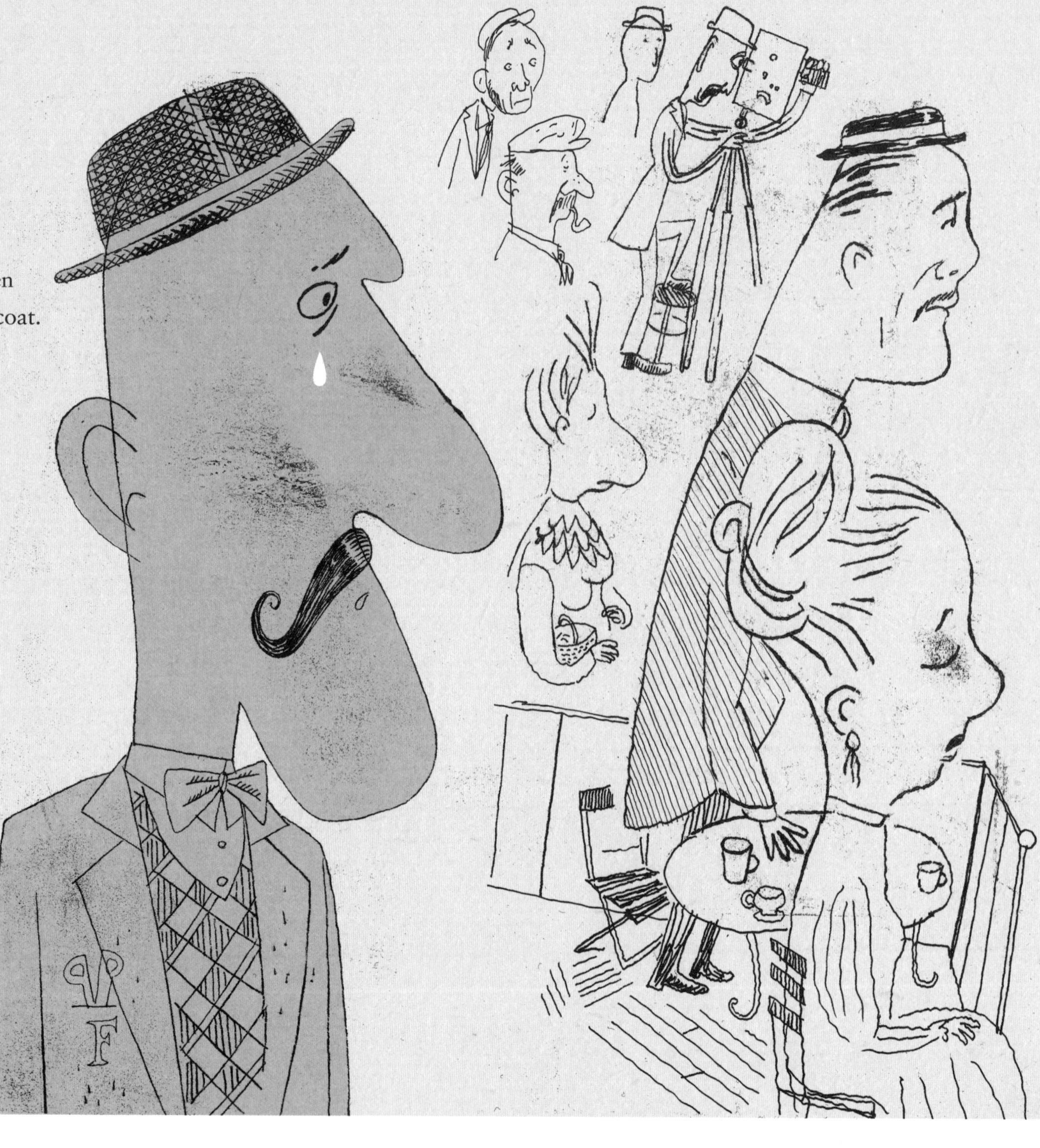

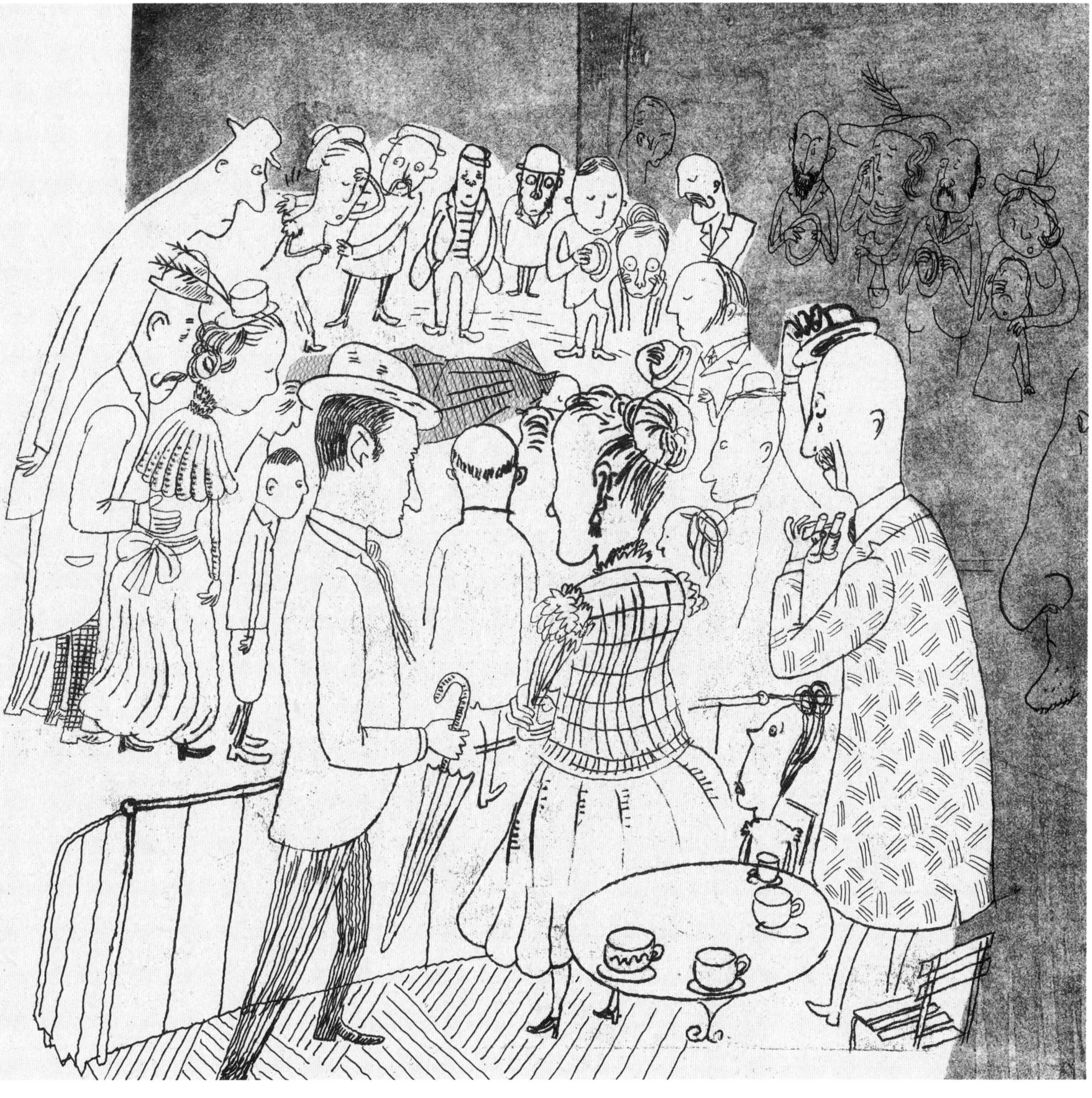

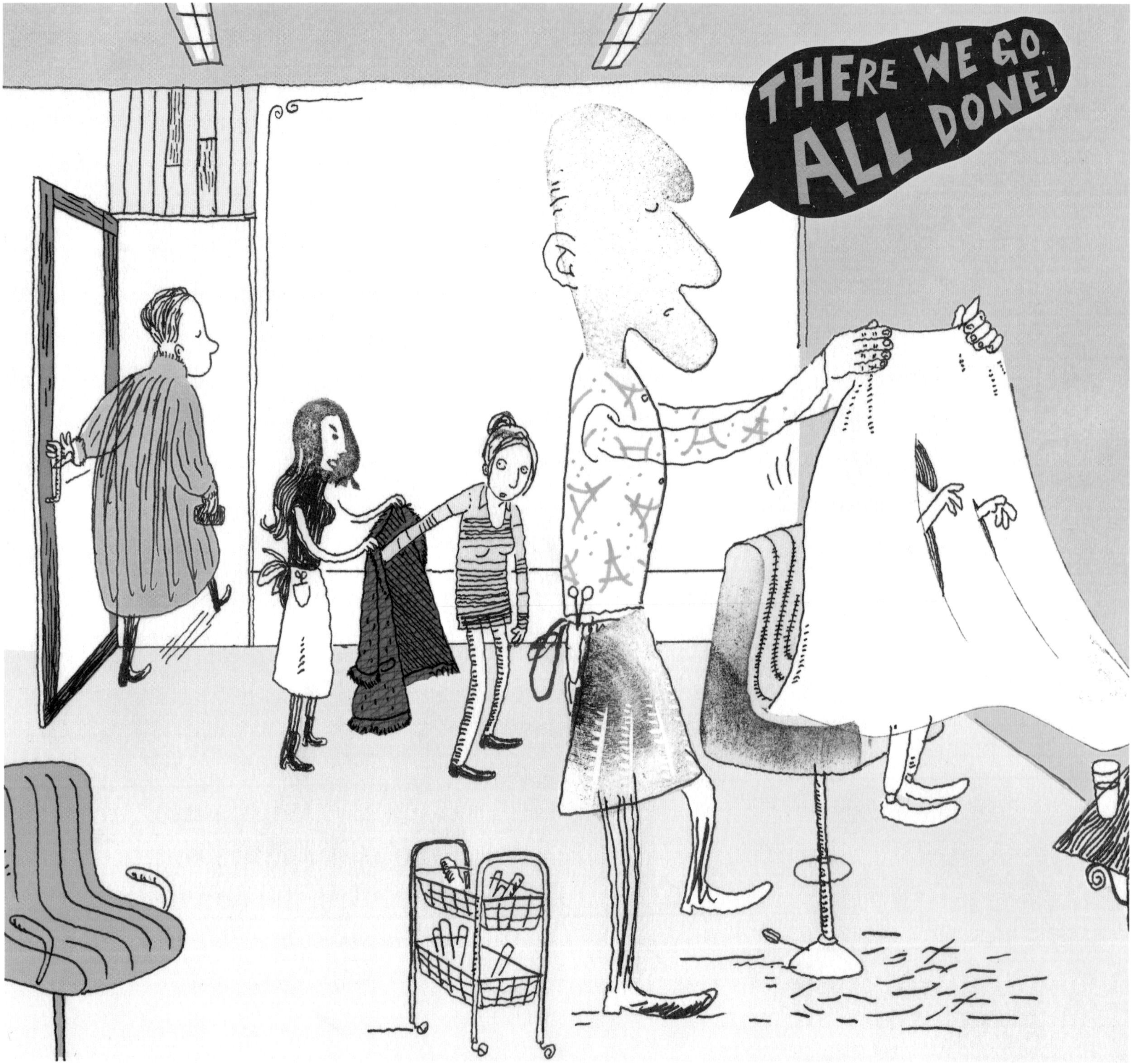
THERE WE GO. ALL DONE!

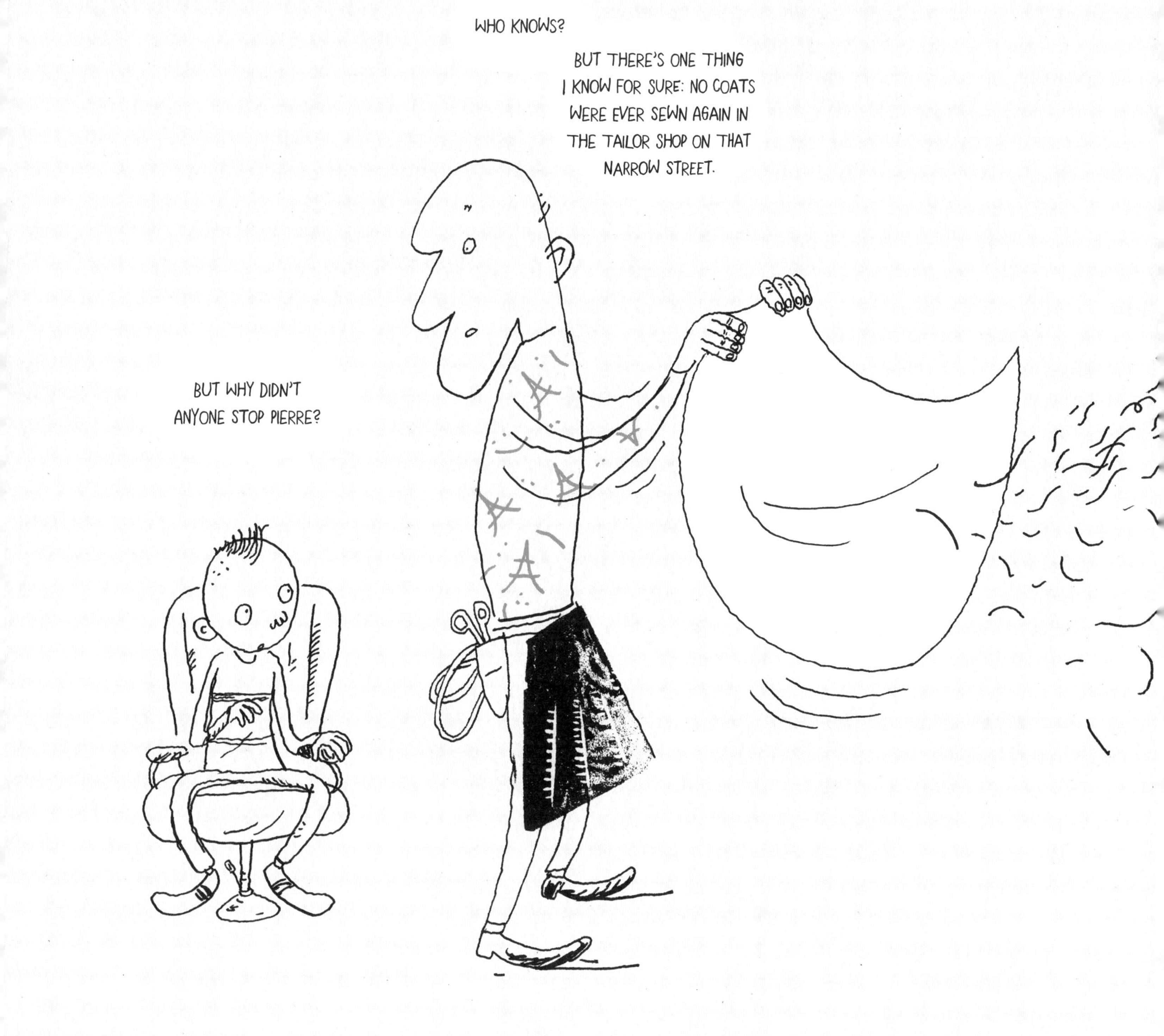
WHO KNOWS?
BUT THERE'S ONE THING I KNOW FOR SURE: NO COATS WERE EVER SEWN AGAIN IN THE TAILOR SHOP ON THAT NARROW STREET.
BUT WHY DIDN'T ANYONE STOP PIERRE?

Instead, François the barber expanded his business.

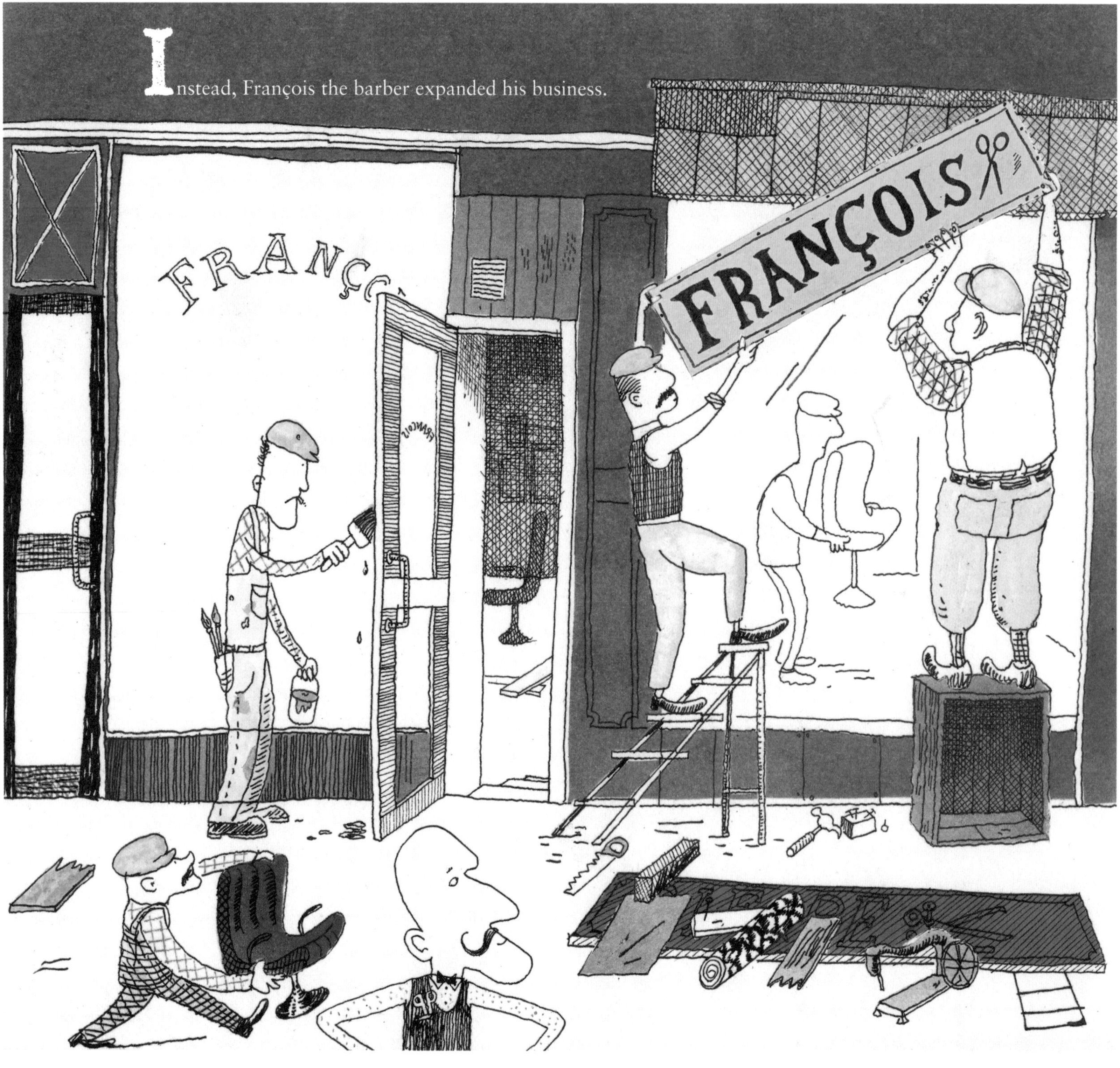
FRANÇOIS

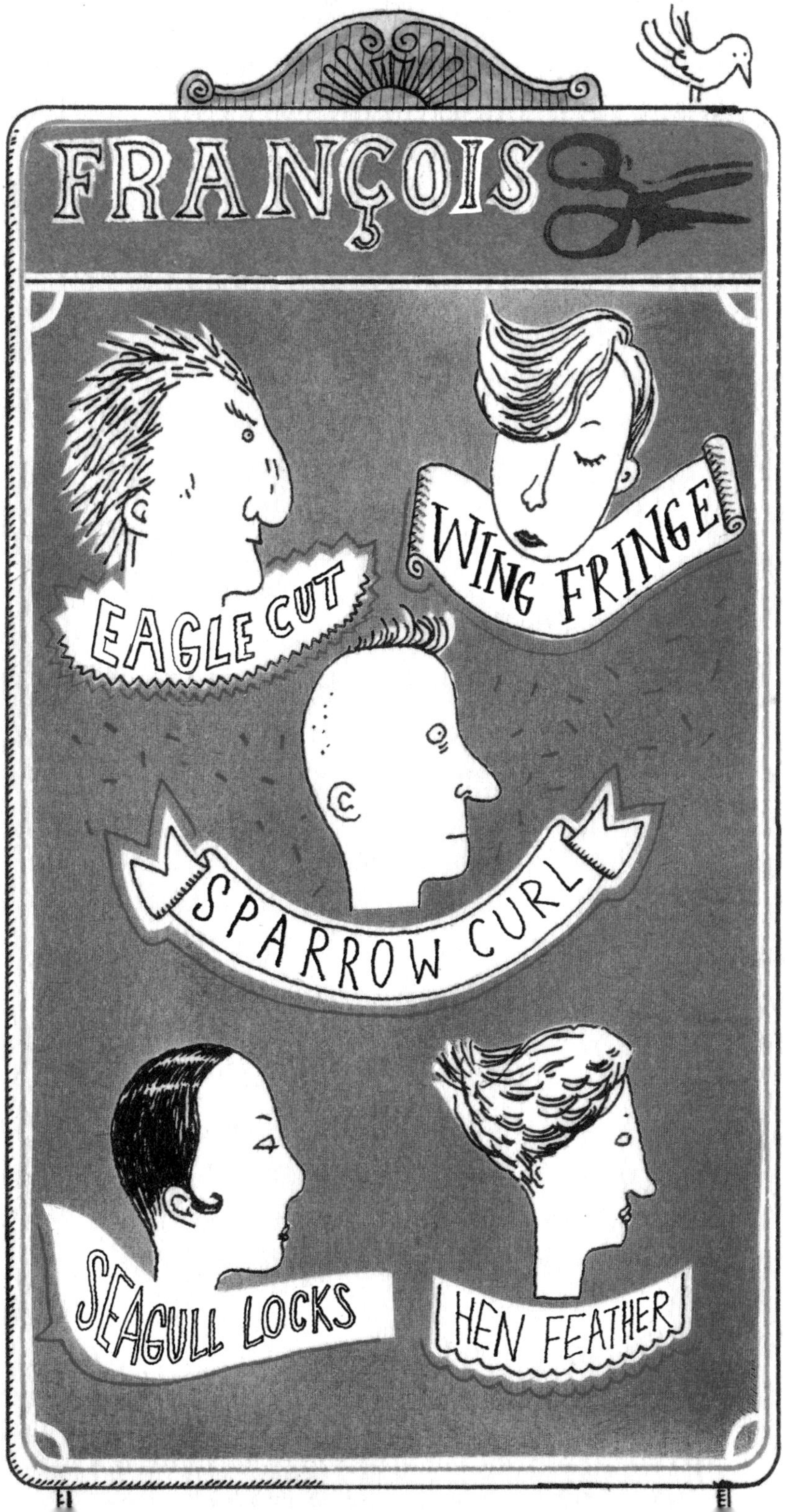
FRANÇOIS
EAGLE CUT
WING FRINGE
SPARROW CURL
SEAGULL LOCKS
HEN FEATHER

He put a portrait of his old friend in a prime place and invented new hairstyles with bird names:
Eagle Cut,
Wing Fringe,
Seagull Locks,
Sparrow Curl

All in honor of Pierre.

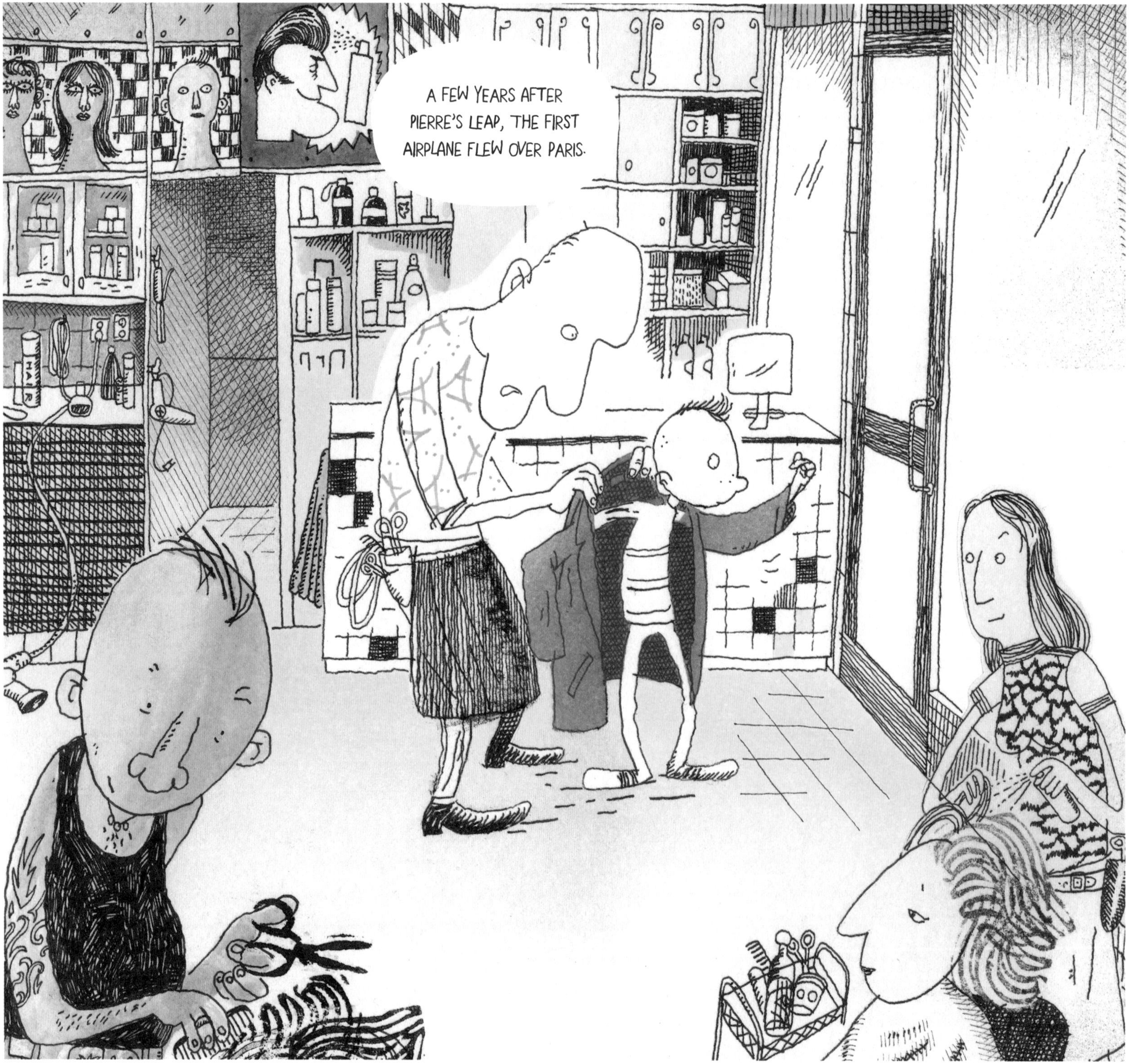
A FEW YEARS AFTER PIERRE'S LEAP, THE FIRST AIRPLANE FLEW OVER PARIS.
HAIR

If only Pierre had been there to see it!

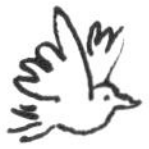

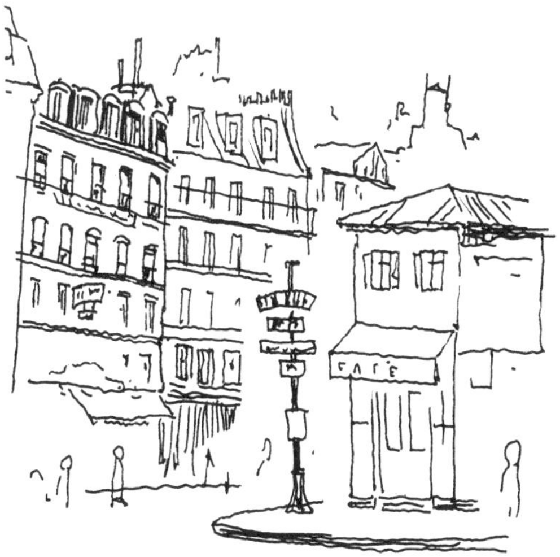
CAFE

Author's Note

When I was a little kid, I was always a bit afraid of children's books dealing with death. They were all so sad, always about children and young people dying. And if they were picture books, the pictures were either gray, dark, and scary; or light, transparent watercolors, where you could almost see the water dripping from the pages, as if they were crying. As a grown-up, I can still remember the heaviness that invaded me when I was little, just from seeing these books in the library. I always turned towards another shelf, looking for the fun, happy books.

Now, some decades later, I've dealt with a lot of loss and grief as an adult, and yes, it can be gray, dark, and scary, as well as filled with enough tears to paint a thousand watercolors. But grief is so much more than that. Grief is a part of life. And what is life? It's everything!

I suppose my own experiences with loss, and the ways in which I've internalized them, are part of why I wrote this story about Pierre and his homemade coat, which couldn't make him the bird he wanted to be. In this story, there is no place for sentimentality, depression, or darkness, even though death arrives. In this story, life goes on.

I wrote *The Bird Coat* intensely one afternoon and evening after stumbling upon a short video clip of the German tailor Franz Reichelt standing on a ledge of the Eiffel Tower, ready to fly wearing his homemade parachute. The first thing that sparked my interest in this story was how odd it was. How very strange, yet how real, too.

The clip was only a few seconds long, and I didn't get much information about what actually had happened, but instantly I knew: This is a story made for a children's book, and all of the things I don't know about the flying tailor, I'll make up myself. And so I did, and I had a lot of fun doing it. Writing should be fun, and digging into this odd story inspired me to write it in a light, carefree way. Finally, I thought it was good enough to submit to a children's book publisher. There was only one question: Was this actually a children's book?

That was a key question, because having your main character die in a very direct and unsentimental way is really not how books for children traditionally deal with death, as I well knew. Still, I couldn't let this hold me back, because if no one pushes the limits of literature and art, nothing new will ever happen. If no one breaks the rules, there will never be anything to discuss or think about, and there will be no new experiences. Everything will be safe and the same. I think literature and art should reflect life. And life is never the same. Life can also push your limits. Life is not always safe. It's full of risk and uncertainty.

The Bird Coat is a book with many layers that pushes a number of limits—limits that have to do with dreams and their pursuit, as well as loss and grief. The form and design of the story are also quite complex: It's a picture book that is a little poetic and a little cartoonish, a little fun and a little sad at the same time, and this complexity can trigger different feelings and reactions in different people. Moreover, the never fully answered question—"Is this actually a children's book?"—will perhaps always stick to the story and add another layer to it. There is luckily no formula for how children's books about death and loss should be written. They may very well be strange and playful like *The Bird Coat*, because grieving always has a strong element of moving forward, of searching for light, even when it's only about getting through the day.

As life is lived, lessons are learned, and I hope some of my own lessons can be passed on to new people who need them, through this book. I will remind you of the hairdresser François, who goes back to work, honoring his friend with some new, fancy hairstyles with bird names. It's as if he were saying: Crying is not forever.

—Inger Marie Kjølstadmyr